INHERITED ISSUES

A SAMANTHA SERIES NOVEL BY

CLAUDIA WHITSITT

Please Visit Ms. Whitsitt at:
Website: www.claudiawhitsitt.com
Facebook: www.facebook.com/claudiawhitsitt
Twitter: twitter.com/claudiawhitsitt
Pinterest: Claudia Whitsitt

INHERITED ISSUES
Copyright 2015 by Claudia Whitsitt
Published in the United States by Twisted Vines Press
Print ISBN-13: 978-0-9963436-0-2
ebook ISBN: 978-0-9963436-1-9

Cover Design by Littera Designs
www.litteradesigns.com
Book Formatting by White Hot Formatting

This is a work of fiction. Names, characters, places, and incidents either are the product of the author's imagination or are used fictitiously, and any resemblance to actual persons, living or dead, businesses, companies, events, or locales is entirely coincidental.

BOOKS BY CLAUDIA WHITSITT

THE SAMANTHA SERIES
IDENTITY ISSUES (BOOK 1)
INTIMACY ISSUES (BOOK 2)
INTERNAL ISSUES (BOOK 3)

THE WRONG GUY
BETWEEN THE LINES

All books are available in both print and eBook
formats at your online retailers.

ACKNOWLEDGEMENTS

Special thanks to every one of my supporters, encouragers, and cheerleaders, especially my husband, Don, and my children, Melissa, Noah, and Jenna. My gratitude also goes out to the entire Southern California Writers Conference community, with special hugs to Jennifer Silva Redmond, Michael Steven Gregory, Gayle Carline, and Jeremy Lee James.

There aren't words to express my gratitude to Lori LaBoe for her reads of endless drafts and her steady presence in my life. You rock, BFF!

Last, but never least, thank you to my readers for waiting with anticipation for the next installment in The Samantha Series and for believing in Samantha!

DEDICATION

For Melissa, a most precious light in my life.

CHAPTER ONE

MAYBE AMNESIA—the required starting over, the perpetual clean slate—promotes flexibility and allows the afflicted to become malleable—in ways they never could have been before the injury.

This was certainly the case with my formerly high-strung lover. A year ago, the detective climbed out of his skin when he didn't have all the answers. Now, not only did he no longer care about the answers, he had very few questions.

If I were a confirmed bachelor, I never could have moved in with a virtual stranger and her five kids. The activity quotient alone would have caused me to wrap my toes cliffside. Plus, my anal-retentive self would have been on a full-out campaign to reestablish myself—both my career and my identity. I'd have been clambering onto every psychiatrist's doorstep, forcing my way into doctor's offices and demanding they share all their tricks—hypnotism, cognitive rewiring, 2.4 micrograms of vitamin B12 three times daily and whatever else. I would have done anything so I could have my life back. Whether or not my former life was a good one.

But that's me.

McGrath's doctors reiterated: "Let him regain his memory gradually. Don't try to trigger memories. Give him time. Things should even out."

Eleven months had passed. Holding out hope for a full recovery seemed futile.

I stirred the simmering spaghetti sauce as McGrath's hand traced the curve of my spine. He nestled his nose in the crook of my neck. "You smell delicious."

"It's the sauce, sweetie, not me."

"No," he said, "it's you."

My head fell onto his shoulder and I nuzzled his cheek. He had this way about him. And then some. I turned down the heat on the burner, then tossed the last of the cut veggies into the salad bowl and followed up with, "Let's take a trip."

He scrubbed his hand over his jaw. "I like trips."

"I know you don't remember, but we were travel companions once, and quite compatible."

He offered me his classic dimple-bracketed smile, then laced his fingers with mine and kissed my knuckles. "You've alluded to that trip so many times. When are you going to give me the details?"

I offered him the Reader's Digest version of our trip to Japan, mentioning the drive through the mountains, the two of us giggling like fools at the fertility temple, but omitting how we'd unearthed the mystery around my husband's death and ultimately rid ourselves of the impostor who'd spent years tormenting my family. I reminded him of our dips in the hot springs and how we'd made mad passionate love on Tatami mats at the quaint inn overlooking the sea.

"Sounds like me."

I shot him a knowing glance. "I'm thinking Maine," I continued, accelerating my words. "We could hike in Acadia National Park. I've Googled it— there are fabulous trails through the mountains and along the seashore. We can bike and swim. Eat good food. Stay at peaceful spots."

"When, and for how long?"

"Summer break is right around the corner. We can spend as much time as we like. I found an inn on the outskirts of Bar Harbor. There's a beautiful deck overlooking the ocean. We'll watch the lobster boats putt by, sip a nice cabernet or three, and make mad passionate love."

"Don't know if I can afford the time away," McGrath teased.

I leaned over and kissed his cheek.

"Kids included?"

"Just you and me. Ed wants to take them to the cottage."

Ed, my father-in-law, had remarried a few months back. He and his new wife, Helen, had offered us a break. My kids were overjoyed at any prospect of spending time Up North with their grandfather. They'd spent many summer vacations there—the thought of a few weeks on the beach would hold tons of appeal.

McGrath tapped my fanny. "Sign me up."

"I'll make the reservations."

Of course, I hadn't shared that Southwest Harbor, on the edge of Mount Desert Island, boasted one of the premiere bird-carving museums in the nation. Back in his former life, along with being a head-down, single-minded detective, McGrath had also been a wood carver. He told me that he'd taken up carving in order to keep from drinking to excess, a hazard of his profession. As a result of the shooting, he didn't remember he'd carved the exquisite ducks that sat on his mantle in his quaint little bungalow on the river.

Last week, I'd phoned the Wendell Gilley Museum on my lunch hour and explained our situation. The carver-in-residence, Ben Carlson, described himself as a lifelong birder, and relayed his resume—a degree in biology from the University of Maine, an artist since college. He often taught private classes and he'd be happy to spend mornings with McGrath during our stay. His dad had been a cop, and he was only too happy to help out.

I'd discovered where McGrath's tools were stored and planned to pack them into my overnight bag.

Maybe once he visited the museum where I'd signed him up for carving sessions, the act of holding a dogleg chisel in his sturdy hands would spark a memory.

The special education teacher in me wanted him to be whole again—I couldn't help it. I prayed for a winning memory ticket, crossed all my appendages, and wished the act of carving again would bring McGrath back to me in all his fullness and glory. I told my friend Di about my master plan that afternoon when we speed-walked five miles through our little town.

"You need to stop scheming," she said. "It's not your job to save him."

"You sound like Jack. You two always gang up on me."

"Think, Sam. You're an enabler. You take on all the world's problems as if they're your own."

"And you don't? Adopting two adolescent boys seems like the same type of drastic world-problem-solving measure to me."

"We've both adopted kids—taking in children is giving back, counting our blessings and sharing them with others. Fixing McGrath is not the same thing."

I grabbed Di as she darted into the street, oblivious to the approaching car.

"Thanks," she murmured. "And McGrath's happy. You're imposing your wishes on him. He's not asking you to help him rediscover his past. He's happy with you and the kids. He's created a new life for himself."

"I want him to have a fulfilling life. One with purpose and meaning."

"He already does." Di arched her brows. "I don't know why I'm trying to change you. You're hopeless."

"True." I dabbed at the sweat trickling down my temple. Enabling was involuntary for me, like breathing, or blinking. With that came inevitable consequences—unhealthy ones—like creating people's dependence on me. I dreaded the possible repercussions, but was hard-pressed to change my ways.

"Go to Maine and have a good time. You're way more concerned about McGrath's memory returning than he is, and you know the more time passes, the less chance there is he'll recover much of his past. He's happy. Leave him alone."

Not in my DNA.

CHAPTER TWO

❝WHY DO YOU insist on calling so late at night?" Judy hissed into the phone.

"I have news about Dad's death," Kyle said. "I thought for once, considering I've found his killers, you'd be pleased to hear from me. You know I wouldn't call this late unless I had news."

Right. In the two years since the murder, Kyle called whenever he'd been drinking, crying about Dad and vowing he'd never rest until he saw their father's killer brought to justice. As far as Judy was concerned, Dad's involvement in her life was over some fifteen years ago—the first time he died—and whether or not this last death was real made no difference to her. Whatsoever. But Kyle still fought to fill the void of growing up with an absent father, hoping, even after death, he could finally be interesting enough for Dad to come around.

Though Dad was no prize, Judy had loved him, as any daughter loves her dad, but she'd grown to recognize him for what he was, a criminal in a business suit. And not only a highfalutin embezzler, but a hired assassin who was willing to work for anyone with the right amount of cash. Sadly, her brother had inherited more than his father's good looks and charm.

"I've told you a gazillion times, Kyle. I believe the State Department. Their final word was that Dad died in the line of duty. I got on with my life long ago and put him to rest. You're wasting your life on vengeance, and to what end?"

"This end. I'm trying to tell you. I figured out who killed him, and you'll never believe what I'm about to tell you."

Judy blew out her breath and sank into a kitchen chair, resting her forehead on her hand. If she just let him have his say, she'd be back in bed before long. "What did you find out?"

"A woman killed him. She was trying to uncover the details of her husband's murder, and decided Dad was to blame. She set him up, lured him to a deserted inn in Japan, then had her cop boyfriend shoot him before she finished him off with a tire iron."

Kyle was silent for a long moment. "I've found her. She's a teacher—if you can believe that—and she lives in a small town in the Midwest. Lexington, Michigan. I'm willing to meet you there and talk to her. Confront her. I thought about calling the authorities, but I'd rather handle this on our own.

"I don't trust the law."

Poor Kyle. His childhood had been a mess. When Dad left Toronto for the States, he'd dumped his love interest—improbably named Chastity—leaving her six months pregnant, penniless, and on the hunt for her next sugar daddy. Problem was, her idea of a sugar daddy was someone who could supply her with a steady diet of heroin, cigarettes, and junk food. Being the oldest, Judy had met Chastity several times, and couldn't help but want to rescue Kyle when the little tyke arrived three months later. She offered babysitting services whenever she could, and even talked her own mom into letting Kyle stay with them when Chastity ran off with the flavor of the month.

"I wish you would come for a visit. We have tons of room."

"Sure you do." His voice was sharp, disapproving. "Since you married the rich guy."

Judy rolled her eyes and stepped over to the coffee pot. This would be a long, drawn-out call, and she needed her wits about her to dissuade her impulsive hooligan half-brother from doing anything rash. In the past, his talk was just talk, but now he had someone in his crosshairs, and she needed to talk him down, fast.

"Let's strategize. Sort things out. I want to see the evidence. I'm not wrong in assuming you have photographs and documentation, am I? And I need time to wrap my head around the next step. Please come. Where are you now? Chicago?"

"I don't want to tell you where I'm staying. My luck, you'll call the cops and tell them I'm a crazy loon who needs to be put away for the public's protection. And, yes, I have proof."

"I haven't seen you since Christmas. The weather is fantastic. We've had 75 degrees every day this week. Bright sunshine too. I'll take you to the Laurentians and we'll go mountain biking."

Judy had learned when her brother was young that his ADD was best served with outdoor time. Nature calmed him in a way neither medication nor stiff discipline could. A bike trip to the mountains would give her time to settle him down, and hopefully she'd be able to convince him, once and for all, to let go of the ridiculous notion that he needed to avenge their father's death.

"Come on, Kyle, the kids have been asking when you're coming to take them fishing this summer. Come now, you can show me what you've found out about Dad, and we can make some decisions about how to handle the information."

A long moment of silence met her words. "Are you trying to trick me?"

Great. Now he was paranoid as well.

"No, I don't have an angle. Look, if you want me to be a part of this, come. If not, take your information to the authorities, and let them handle this. I understand your need for closure, and I'd love to be able to help you, but you can't have it both ways. I can't come to you because you won't tell me where you are. You can come to me, but I can't force you. Please, don't make this difficult. I have the entire summer open. Plan your trip. I'll be waiting."

"Fine, I'll be there in a few weeks. I have a couple of jobs to finish before I can leave town."

Judy's heart caught in her chest. She feigned excitement. "Great, I can't wait to see you, and the boys will be overjoyed."

She fixed her eyes on the clock, blinked, and tried to bring the time into focus. Four in the morning. She shut off the coffee pot and dragged herself up the stairs and back to bed.

***

Once he ended the call, Kyle gathered what little information he had. Samantha Stitsill taught special education. He hated special education teachers. His mom had always tried to "get him serviced" like he was a car with a blinking engine light. And his teachers at school always threatened to send him to the special education classroom for a "time out."

Such a productive way of handling kids who struggled to learn, kick them out of the classroom and send them to the cubbyhole where crazy schizos rocked in their chairs and no one learned a goddamn thing. Made perfect sense to him.

He tucked the article he had printed off the

Internet, which reported the woman's cop boyfriend's shooting a year ago, into his briefcase. His name was James McGrath, and he'd sustained some permanent brain damage, according to what Kyle read. Couldn't have happened to a nicer guy.

Armed with his printed material and photos of both Samantha Stitsill and James McGrath he'd secured from a Google search, he began to pack his bags. Before trekking all the way to Montreal though, he'd drive to southeastern Michigan, see Samantha with his own eyes, and conduct a personal assessment of Detective McGrath's permanent injuries, just to be sure.

And yes, there were those jobs to finish along the way. He already had those plans mapped out. Bang. Bang.

CHAPTER THREE

I DROVE TO McGrath's place after work. His carving tools were tucked away in the garage, as expected, in the cabinet above his tool bench. Beneath the clamshell pine case, I caught the glint of a familiar container; a metal lockbox resembling the one I had handed over to him two years ago. He told me then he would deliver the contents, a collection of passports and receipts for successful assassinations which my husband's impostor had committed, over to the proper authorities.

The hair on my arms stood on end. I shifted the latch and my heartbeat quickened.

Inside were old gun shells. The nagging image of my late husband's passport photo tugged at my brain and I dumped the contents onto the bench. From beneath the casings fell two passports. I shivered in spite of the stifling heat and opened one. My fingers trembled as I gaped at Jon Stitsill's photograph. This man had stolen my husband's identity, killed him— and my dog—and tried to kill McGrath and me the summer before last. Because of McGrath's skill with a weapon, Stitsill no longer posed a threat, but fear shuddered through me just the same. Despite my trembling fingers, I leafed through the pages, checking the country stamps. Botswana. Mexico. The States. Japan. Russia.

As I'd learned last year in Japan, Jon's boss had ties to the Russian mob.

The air turned to ice. I couldn't stop shaking. As I turned the final passport page, a narrow slip of folded paper fell to the floor. I retrieved and opened it. A receipt with a single name and a dollar amount. I slipped both passports and the receipt inside the zippered pocket of my purse.

If I were McGrath, I would have kept these items for one of two reasons: insurance, or proof of the impostor's past.

So there, Di. I'm not an enabler, I'm a puzzle solver.

The passports provided a logical reason for my insistence on McGrath regaining his memory. My mission was no longer one of projection, but of closure. Both McGrath and I were involved in the case, and every cop likes to wrap up a mystery with a tidy little bow. Once his memory returned, he could explain the presence of these passports. With his past restored, the world would be right.

Sure. Because life works that way.

After I replaced the metal box on the shelf, I

toted the toolbox to my van and placed the kit in the back seat, then pressed the lock button on the remote. I rubbed my arms to warm them, but my efforts were fruitless—goose bumps peppered my flesh. I'd place the passports and receipts in my safe deposit box at the bank on the way home. For safekeeping.

***

As McGrath drove from Bangor to Bar Harbor, I relaxed in the passenger seat and allowed my shoulders to drop. I should have suggested we get away a long time ago.

Seeing McGrath behind the wheel of our rented fire-engine-red Fiat, tooling down Route 3, rambling on about the lobster pounds he'd investigated along our route, did my heart good. He seemed like his old self. In charge. Confident. And sexy as ever.

McGrath seemed back in his element somehow, yet I couldn't quite reason why, so I gazed out my open window, taking in the leaping green rises of the earth and the azure blue of the sea. My mantra became: relax, let life happen, give up control.

Not easy for a girl like me—I'd been in charge of my own birth family for years, then again with my own two kids after I'd been stupid enough to marry an alcoholic and think I could reform him. Little old me. Forgetting to learn from my mistakes. After my subsequent divorce, when Jon came along, I knew I'd hit the big leagues. He had a college degree, a fast-track career, and two kids, just like me. We had enough dough to support our children and sock away money for their college educations. Only bad thing, he travelled more often than not, so the five kids were mostly left to me. Not his fault, just his job.

I did what came naturally—coordinating schedules, mediating disputes, maintaining our home, doing laundry, cooking, making sure homework was completed, in full and on time. And then I had my own full-time teaching job.

Give up the resentment, Sam, I warned myself for the umpteenth time.

The car veered to the right and I realized McGrath had been talking to me the entire time I'd been lost inside my head. He pulled into a lobster pound in the town of Trenton. The quaint little place with a giant cut-out of the familiar red crustacean was accented by cisterns of boiling water lined up along one side of the storefront, along with picnic tables, their red checkered tablecloths glinting beneath a huge crimson awning on the other side. The smell of melted butter was nothing less than intoxicating.

I stepped out of the car and salty air filled my senses. My blood pressure dropped a full ten degrees and if McGrath hadn't reached for my hand and ushered me inside, I might have stood there for hours, simply breathing in and out.

We each ordered lobster, mine a standard 1¼

pounds, his a whopping 2 pounder.

"Do they call this place a pound because you order by the pound?" His eyes glinted with good humor.

"I think it's more like a dog pound," I countered.

It didn't matter which of us was right, we added two buttered ears of corn and cole slaw to our order and headed outside. A group of seniors sat at the table next to us. They passed around adult beverages from a cooler. Obviously, they were seasoned patrons and knew the drill.

"We have so much to learn," I said.

"You, my dear," McGrath replied, "are a natural born detective."

By the time our order number was called and he jogged inside to retrieve our food, we were both famished. We cracked claws, dipped rich sweet meat in salted butter, and moaned with sheer delight.

Another couple joined our table, offering us a couple of beers, which we gratefully accepted. They asked the usual getting-to-know-you questions. Where are you from? What do you do?

After I shared details of my teaching career, and the fact that my five kids kept me out of trouble, I held my breath and waited.

McGrath patted my hand with warm affection, the twinkle in his eyes even more pronounced. His shoulders squared, and his chest puffed out as he spoke. "I'm a detective for a local police force near where we live. I'm fortunate enough to have a little R&R time so my sweetie and I could get away."

This was the first time I'd heard him utter words relating to his career since the shooting. The department had strongly suggested a medical retirement as his best option considering he wasn't fit for duty. But this sounded like he hadn't yet given up on his career. My heart took flight.

After the couple left and we deposited our shell-filled trays into the garbage can next to the wash-up sink, I broached the subject with him. "Do you want to go back to work?"

"Not sure," he answered.

"Makes sense." I waited to see if he would say more.

A long moment passed. "How much do I need to remember? I'm sick of meeting with the department shrink. I'm the same guy I was before the shooting, aren't I?"

I spent a long moment constructing my answer. "You're mellower."

"What do you mean?" He peered at me as if I were the keeper of a secret code, one that would somehow unlock his cell door.

I patted his hand. "You're focused on other things right now. Not a bad thing, but you dove headfirst into the kids and me. From a personal standpoint, I can't tell you how grateful I am. Without you, my life would be a total mess. With you, my family functions like a BMW, smooth as silk with little to no road noise."

"So you're saying something is missing from my life."

I offered him a sympathetic grin. "Not my place to say or to know. The way I see things, you were given the chance to start over. Do whatever you like. You took life in a new direction. I envy you the opportunity."

"What would you change if you could?" he asked.

"We're not talking about me," I pointed out, shifting uncomfortably in my seat.

"Will you marry me?"

I swallowed hard. "I hadn't expected a proposal so early in the trip."

Quiet, and clearly a little disheartened, McGrath rolled back onto Route 3 toward our hotel.

"Let's get settled in our room and see a few sights before we make any major decisions."

Twenty minutes later, we checked into our room in a Victorian-fashioned mansion smack dab on the shore of the Atlantic. After we unpacked, we meandered to the veranda overlooking the harbor. Lobster boats collected their catches and a sailboat skimmed over the smooth water. We lounged in the Adirondack chairs on the deck and held hands. The cloudless sky bathed us in sunshine. The air, fresh and salty, relaxed us.

I lolled my head back and closed my eyes. I wanted to marry him. I couldn't envision a life without him. But my heartbeat galloped like a thoroughbred at the starting gun when he'd popped the question. If only I could stop over-thinking things. I loved the man. He was great with my kids. My agenda—getting his memory back before we made a decision to marry—wasn't his agenda. If he was content with his life, it wasn't my place to push him into more.

He squeezed my hand. "Anybody home?"

I softened at the touch of his hand on mine. "Let's wander into town and see the sights."

"Deal."

As we slipped on our tennies in anticipation of the two-mile trek to town, I noticed a laminated menu on the coffee table. I perused the choices before turning over the placard. On the back, the story of the inn was told in simple, abbreviated form. The mansion's original owner, Arthur Edinborough, had been a loner who'd struck it rich. In his later years, around age forty, he'd traveled to Europe and met the girl of his dreams. He brought her back to Maine, moved her into the mansion, and there she raised their five children while he traveled extensively for business.

After Arthur's oldest daughter married, at the age of twenty, he was found murdered in his home while the rest of the family was away on vacation. Law officials initially conjectured that he was mistaken for someone else and his murder-for-hire was a hit gone wrong. Then, they got wind of some family discourse. His son-in-law, the prime suspect in the slaying, was eventually acquitted. The true killer was never found.

"Jon, look at this." I handed him the card.

McGrath stared at me until the realization hit me. I'd just called him Jon.

"I don't know where that came from," I said. "Forgive me?" I'd never called him by Jon's name before.

He ignored me and read quietly for a few moments. "Striking similarities."

"What do you mean?" I narrowed my eyes in hopes that I wouldn't miss a single nuance. I swear to God, I could almost see Tinker Bell above his head, sprinkling magical memory dust. I hoped my blunder had been overlooked by his keen interest in the reading. Hurting McGrath was on the bottom of my list.

"The story must remind you of Jon. The traveling. The five kids. The murder." He scratched his head.

I'd worked with enough brain-damaged individuals in my career to realize nothing good would come of my filling in the blanks. Plus, the doctor's words echoed in my brain, "In order for him to become whole again, he had to remember."

I waited for an excruciatingly long moment. He

finally continued. "When we went to Japan to sort out Jon's murder, I wondered for a brief time if his death might have been a mistake. If someone had confused him with the impostor. I also wondered if he'd been killed because Mr. Bredel suspected him of being the low-down jerk from Botswana who had abandoned his pregnant daughter. Bredel was an insistent bastard and could have been seeking revenge on his own, you know?"

Inside, I hopped up and down like I was riding a pogo stick, but feared if I rejoiced, said out loud that he was remembering, I'd somehow jinx his memories and he'd forget everything. I tried to calm myself. Just because he remembered a little didn't mean he'd remember everything.

If he did remember everything, he might remember the trouble we'd gone through before his shooting and be disappointed in me. Or question if I truly wanted to be with him—he might worry I'd taken him in like a stray dog, and embraced his recovery as my personal mission because I pitied him.

My inner ramblings confirmed my suspicions. I needed a shrink way more than he did. My neurosis was out of control.

I swallowed hard and allowed my instincts to take over. "You really thought Bredel might be behind Jon's murder? You never said so."

"As a detective, I considered every possibility. I also made decisions on what did and didn't make sense to share with you. You'd been through so much—I decided to follow your lead during the trip. I wasn't involved in an official way, if you recall. I was there to lend support, offer my professional opinion, and not divulge every crazy scenario that ran through my head. If at some point something undeniably pertinent occurred to me, I would have told you. Plus, I was hoping to get you in the sack. If I spent too much time mulling things over with you, we never would have had any time for …"

"For?"

His dimples deepened as he smiled. "Lovin', baby. Sweet, sweet lovin'."

I wanted to pepper him with questions about what else he remembered, but his grin screamed *take me now.* So we took advantage of having the most romantic room in the inn.

CHAPTER FOUR

AFRAID TO BREAK the magic memory spell, I lay in the stillness of McGrath's arms and reveled in the wash of his breath on my neck. As he slept, I inhaled his spicy scent. I said a silent prayer and hoped sleep would further strengthen his recollections. He was coming back to me. Whole again.

I cautioned myself not to become optimistic too quickly—the heartbreak would be devastating—and gazed at the ceiling. Sunlight painted swaths of shadow and light on the flowery lace canopy draped atop the four-poster bed. Shadows and light had been the theme of my life. Like any intelligent person, I preferred the light, but the shadows had forced me to become the strong, independent woman I now was. Widowed a few months shy of my fortieth birthday, and left with five children to raise. To say nothing of the fact I'd shot and killed an intruder in my own home. Within six months of my husband's death, I'd lost my mother-in-law. And my son suffered a traumatic brain injury a year later. It seemed impossible.

McGrath's remembering indicated a period of light had entered my life again, and I was humbled, grateful, and hopeful. With his memories and my determination, we could become the authors of our own life. Trite, but this is how my brain works. My heart quickened with anticipation.

He slept for a few minutes more, then kissed my forehead and snuggled against me. Our day was destined to be one of reconnection. I rose from the bed and poured two goblets of wine, pulled up some music on my iPhone, and climbed the staircase back into the raised bed. I handed McGrath his wine, clinked his glass, and sipped my own as I sat Indian style in front of him.

"I wish you were dressed," McGrath said.

"What?" My jaw dropped.

"You know I love undoing buttons." His laughter carried a melody, like music.

"The elevator." I sat, stunned. McGrath had undressed me in the elevator when we'd been in Japan, undone my round, silk-covered buttons one by one. "You defrocked me," I teased.

Oh Tinker Bell, I prayed, sprinkle more magic dust. Please.

His fingertips played over my curves. "The small of your back is my favorite part of this fabulous anatomy."

"My body, your favorite. Your body, mine."

"I remember the inn on the cliffs. When Stitsill showed up. I've never been so afraid in my life. If something would have happened to you…"

"We've survived a disaster movie, haven't we?" I caressed the hair on his arm as he traced a freckle on my cheek.

He wrinkled his brow. "I feel different."

"You're getting your life back. Do you feel better, or just different?"

"Kind of like I just finished eating a juicy steak. I'm full, but not satiated. Satisfied, though. Down to my core."

I stuck out my bottom lip in a pout. "I thought our love-making caused your only supreme contentment."

"There's that." He became pensive, twirling a lock of my hair into a curl, then a flush of anxiety covered his face.

I grasped his hand and locked eyes with him. "I'll be with you every step of the way."

"I'm a bit unnerved, remembering and all."

"The shock is bound to be unsettling. Take deep breaths."

"Will regaining my memory always be like this? Remembering in stops and starts? Maybe my past will flash before my eyes all at once. Wait. How will I know if I've remembered everything?"

"I'm not sure, but I know you and I know you

like to have a plan. There's no plan here. You'll be required to exercise patience. Not a strong suit for you."

He mustered a grin. "Sounds like a warning."

"I know you pretty well," I said.

"Probably better than I know myself. If your assessment of me is correct, the process of remembering may make me pretty crazy."

"We've waited a short eternity for this. Let's enjoy the moment and not get ahead of ourselves." I leaned into him as I set my wine glass on the nightstand, my breasts pressing against his muscled chest as I did. I brushed my lips against his and let my tongue slip between them, teasing, tasting.

McGrath drew me against his chest, nuzzling my head and inhaling the scent of my hair.

"In the meantime," I said, "let's get some exercise."

The warmth of my body against his worked its usual magic. Two sweaty bodies later, we showered, dressed, and then headed into town.

The quaint inns lining the highway, the distant view of the ocean, and the heavily wooded grounds provided all the ingredients for a steady diet of romance. McGrath squeezed my hand in his and I faced him as he framed my cheeks with his warm palms.

"I have a personal agenda for our trip," he

said, kissing me gently at first, then with added fervor.

"Our room is just down the road," I teased. " Shall we head back?"

"No need," he said. "Just want you to know how much I love you."

I glanced at my watch. We'd only been in Maine for three hours. "So far, this trip has been perfect. You're starting to remember your past, we've made mad passionate love, and you're professing your love for me on a regular basis. Can't get much better than this."

"It's weird," he said. "Remembering is clearing my head. Doesn't even make sense."

"In my experience, life rarely makes sense."

"I don't want to let go of you. Thinking about Japan, about your being alone with Stitsill while I was trapped inside the inn, the thought of losing you those memories are bringing my life into focus"

"You've never been the sentimental type. Not really. Is your personality changing, too?"

"Maybe I could use some changing. The more I remember, the more I question myself."

I narrowed my eyes. "You're a perfectly decent human being. Always have been. Always will be. Telling me that you love me is new, but I've always known how you felt about me. One of the things I love most about you is that you show me all the time. Like I teach my kids in writing class, 'show, don't tell,'" I paused to stroke his cheek. "You do so much for me. I love knowing you have my back. The way you've adopted my kids, helped with practical things like the dishes and the laundry. Trust me, your actions speak volumes."

"And you've cared for me, never wanting anything in return. Welcomed my loser, memory-less, jobless self into your home and your family without a single hesitation. That's love."

"Okay." His depth of feeling unnerved me. " We've established we're good for each other."

He stopped me again. "Marry me."

I gazed into his baby blues and was overtaken by some centrifugal force. "In due time," I answered, not knowing where the words had come from, but guessing my agreement came from the deepest recesses of my soul. And now that my answer was out there, I could hardly take it back. At least I'd given myself a cushion.

McGrath looked shocked. While he'd never been one to whisper sweet nothings into my ear, he'd asked that particular question so many times, I'd lost count. A smile grew across his face, his eyes sparkled, and his dimples deepened. He swung my arm, quickened his pace to a near run, and practically dragged me down the street. "This," he said, "is a very good day."

We virtually skipped the last mile to town, stopping briefly to revel at the shops, inns, and restaurants seasoning the streets. In the distance the sun danced on the water, and in between the sailing ships and the lobster boats, we promised each other a leisurely walk along the shore, right after we celebrated our engagement with a chilled mug of beer.

We ducked inside a new Irish Pub on the water, and plopped ourselves down at an outside table overlooking the water. We placed our order and toasted the thought of our new life.

"Where should we have the ceremony?"

"Hold your horses," I demanded. "I've just agreed to marry you. What's the rush?"

"Do you want the kids to be in the wedding party? They should be a part of things. Should Nick give you away? He is the 'man of the family' after all. And I should ask him for permission—it would mean the world to me if he'd entrust me with your care."

I laughed. For about five minutes. What the heck had happened to this man? The jarring of his memory had induced a form of ADHD. A hefty supply of Ritalin might be necessary to control his mania.

He eyed me as if I was out of my mind, and I began to seriously worry. Maybe he was actually losing touch. This brain of his, which had been hard-wired with logic for years, might derail, run amuck. His personality might change with this sudden rush of memories. I suddenly wished that I hadn't agreed to marry him, but counseled myself to calm down and enjoy the moment. We weren't getting married right this second. Surely, we'd understand what was happening to him as time went on.

"Hey." McGrath startled me from my runaway thoughts.

"What?" I locked his gaze.

"What are you thinking?"

"Silly things," I admitted, fingering the saltshaker. "I just had an idea."

McGrath leaned over the table and kissed me full out, on the lips. "Do tell."

"Why don't we go into business together?"

"What, you mean like set up a tutoring business? I don't have a teaching degree."

"No, not teaching. Private Investigators." I formed an arc with my hand, the shingle we'd hang over the door. "Just think, we could use our initials. Stitsill and McGrath—S & M Investigations."

His eyes crinkled with good humor. "With a business name like that, we might get arrested. Or at least draw some very unusual clientele."

"I know it's premature," I confessed. "But you've always told me that I have an inquisitive nature, and whether or not you remember, I was helpful in past cases, both yours and mine."

"Wait a minute. The Macchione case. The guy's daughter was your former student."

"Exactly," I answered. "And in the end, she was instrumental in solving her mother's murder. With my help, of course." I smiled coyly, hoping McGrath would settle into the notion eventually. I loved teaching. I really did. But I'd discovered over the past few years a certain delight in working with high functioning individuals, adults even, and I loved solving mysteries.

"You've accused yourself of naïveté in the past. Solving cases isn't easy. And certainly not for amateurs."

"You sound a tad condescending." I averted my eyes and chewed on my bottom lip.

He reached out and clasped my hand. "We're rushing things. Marriage. Changing careers. The lot of it. Can we slow down and enjoy our drinks?"

Now, he was the one to press the brake pedal. "Deal." I raised my glass. "To our future."

CHAPTER FIVE

DNA IS HARD-wired. Even in twins who've been separated at birth. The same held true for Kyle, even though he'd grown up seeing his father on the rarest of occasions—not the expected holidays or weekends for a kid with unattached parents, but rather the odd visit, out of the blue—when he showed up and pulled Kyle out of school for a day or two. They didn't do the regular father-son things like go fishing, play basketball, or build a doghouse, but Kyle did accompany his dad on stakeouts. His dad showed him, in those very few memorable visits, how to hunt. Not deer or birds, but humans. Kyle held tight to those memories and prided himself on being diligent, quite unlike the student he was in the classroom, the prized pupil of his dad.

Dad taught him to focus on details and nuances. He also counseled him in the manipulation of the human spirit. Kyle learned how malleable people could be. Turn on a little charm, and you could predict their next move. A little cuteness and a little kindness was all he needed. Kyle practiced with his teachers at school and kept track of how well the techniques worked, so he could boast when he saw Dad.

Those were the few times when his dad wore a genuine smile, the pride gleaming in his eyes like a lighthouse in the fog. Dad would pat him on the back and say, "Well done, Son." Kyle had never been happier than in those moments and promised himself he would grow up to be just like his dad.

He slicked his hair back like Dad did, and spent time in front of the mirror, mimicking Dad's facial expressions—the ones he used with waitresses in order to get an extra helping, or a free dessert.

Kyle had the same build as his dad. Long and lanky. But instead of using those long arms to shoot hoops when he was in junior high, he practiced picking pockets, and became one of the slickest guys in town. Hell, he could even steal from his teachers, leaving them with no freaking clue Kyle was the culprit.

Kyle was pleased with himself, proud of what he'd become.

Depression was the only thing standing in his way. He supposed he inherited his melancholy from Dad—not all his genes were winning tickets—although Mom suffered her fair share of gloominess with the booze and pills.

His sister Judy had warned him countless times

to stay away from drugs and alcohol—they would be like ingesting poison, she said. But Kyle was never one to heed warnings. His sister was overprotective, and while she meant well, she could be a pain in his ever-loving ass.

Kyle stopped off in Wilmette and finished his first job, icing a middle-aged attorney who'd offended someone. The job went according to plan. The guy lived in a remote area outside of the city, and his wife left for work earlier than he did. Kyle simply knocked on the door, met the guy with a quick and deadly bullet, hopped in the car, and was on his way.

Kyle never asked for particulars. He didn't want facts to muddle his attention to his work, and didn't want any personal connection to either the victim or to his own employer.

This time, on this second job, things would be different. This was personal. He set his GPS for Lexington, Michigan, delighted to see that he'd be meeting Samantha Stitsill in just four hours.

CHAPTER SIX

I LAY AWAKE long into the night, concerned about McGrath's newfound memory. He remembered a lot quickly, but as I dissected his memories, I realized they were all related to his work. Part of me wanted his recollections to remain that way, and I prayed that he wouldn't remember how I'd pulled away from him. I couldn't bear for him to think there was a point at which I didn't want him.

It was never a lack of love or desire. I was scared. Scared of giving my heart to someone new. Scared of getting hurt. Gun shy. When Jon died, I'd been thrust into a web of emotional issues. I questioned his faithfulness and his love. Add the fact I suspected he'd fathered a child not my own, and I was full of distrust, not just concerning my late husband, but about the entire male gender.

In that moment, I realized with startling clarity how deeply I loved McGrath. When he was shot, I had every intention of spending the rest of my life with him. I'd vowed never to let him out of my sight again, but our past might come back to haunt us.

I was over-thinking. Being dramatic. He obviously loved me. We were compatible in every way. Pretty much. The only thing we'd ever argued about was my hesitation to swan dive into our relationship. After Jon died, McGrath waited almost a solid year before contacting me. He had been more than patient. Made perfect sense that he would be revving his engines, ready to go.

The problem with me was, I'd jump in full tilt, then pull back, like an instant replay, constantly poised on the board. I definitely needed daily therapy. But I was busy. I was on vacation.

McGrath had agreed to meet Ben Carlson, the wood carver, in the morning. It made sense to squeeze in a few hours of sleep. I closed my eyes and finally drifted off. It seemed like seconds later the hotel's clock radio blasted high-pitched electronic whines. I reached over McGrath to shut off the droning sound, and stretched for a few moments before heading into the shower.

The walk to the hotel, separated from the inn by two hundred yards of concrete, proved essential. Coffee, albeit bad coffee, was required. I poured four cups, pressed on plastic lids, and hustled back to our room. McGrath had decided to go for a run, so I settled into a chair on the deck and kicked my feet up on the railing. The rocks, the gentle wash of the waves onto the shore, the sun kissing my cheeks, called for tranquility, still I fought the urge every step of the way. My peaceful surroundings beckoned me—to unwind from the past school year, the hectic life of raising five kids and caring for my recovering lover, but relaxation was out of the question.

As if I had an itch that salve couldn't soothe, the need for change brewed inside me. Lack of satisfaction had been a moniker in my life. I'd never been happy with the status quo. My general discontent had prompted my interest in the mystery surrounding my late husband's identity theft. The fact that my inquisitive nature had tossed me headlong into danger had been an unavoidable side effect. Not worthy of making me change my tack. Even after those events had been wrapped up, or I thought they had, I ceased to leave well enough alone.

I'd rushed off to Japan as soon as possible, to find answers to the burning questions that lingered after his death. In retrospect, the trip had been worthwhile. Jon, I decided, had been a good father and a good husband. The best he could be. He'd never intended to leave me husbandless, my children fatherless. And while he may have wavered on his path, I told myself it wasn't for lack of trying. I compromised the truth so that I could live with reality. For a host of reasons, I continued to hold him in high esteem, in order to allow my children to memorialize him as their hero. They were entitled to see him in a favorable light.

So why did I remain at a crossroads? None of

this made sense. My son Nick had recovered from his coma and its physical aftermath. McGrath was recovering his memory. I set my coffee on the patio table and stepped inside to grab my computer. Tilting the screen so that I could see in spite of the sunlight, I Googled "Private Investigators." The thought of a new career—one in which McGrath and I could team up— held so much appeal, I could hardly contain myself.

My search of "certification for Private Investigators" taught me that eighteen course hours were required. If I requested a leave from my teaching position and attended classes full-time, I could be licensed by December. Move over, Sherlock!

Jon's life insurance policy had left the kids and me with enough money for their college and some extras (he was a big deal, after all), and I knew that the district would grant my leave without a fight. I felt like a kid the night before Christmas, excited about the possibilities. McGrath had mentioned more than once that I possessed a nature for crime-solving. Must have been all those jigsaw puzzles I'd pieced together as a kid. That and the Nancy Drew books that had kept me awake far into the night.

McGrath clicked the door open. "Anybody home?" he called.

"Out on the deck," I answered, closing my laptop.

Sweat dripped from his temples and his shirt was drenched. He looked good. Especially those darned dimples.

"Whatcha doin'?" he asked.

I'd tell him later. "Just playing." He'd think I was crazy and worry for my safety, but joining forces seemed like a solid idea to me. We could work cases together, just like we'd been doing before he was shot. Except we'd only accept cases that weren't dangerous.

Yeah, right.

He kissed the top of my head. "I'd better climb in the shower."

"Coffee's on the desk," I offered as I glanced at my watch. "We have an hour before we're due at the museum."

"I'll hurry." McGrath went inside, leaving me to fill out an online application at our local community college and peruse enrollment for fall classes. Once I'd completed that task, I drafted an email to the HR department at my school district. I felt better than I had in ages.

I tied back my hair and brushed on some make-up as McGrath dressed for his woodworking session.

"What are you going to do while I'm with Ben?" he asked.

"The photos of the museum grounds look heavenly and the novel I've brought along is calling my name. I'll find a quiet bench and read, or wander into town and check out the shops. No need to worry about me."

We strolled toward the rental. I offered to drive. Out of guilt, mostly. Jon had always driven on all of our trips. Since his death, little things haunted me. He'd never been afforded the luxury of enjoying the sights in the way the kids and I had. I vowed not to rob McGrath of those simple pleasures. He tossed me the keys without a fight. Jon would never have given in, he'd have insisted on driving. I tucked memories in the back of my mind—in the "think about that later" slot.

I rolled the car south onto Eden St. and then veered west onto Highway 233 through Acadia National Park. Our first view of the park left my mouth agape. A thick forest of pine trees lined the road, and spectacular views of the ocean popped through as we climbed the trail across the mountain. Elegant century-old mansions gave way to the sea, prompting my wayward brain to make up stories of long-ago staff and residents— tunneling through secret passageways for the trysts that keep one's heart alive when living in the middle of nowhere, craving warmth in the depth of a rugged winter. I opened my window and let the sweet scent of the fresh air tickle my nose.

When we arrived at the Gilley Museum, a short twenty-five minutes later, I discovered immaculate grounds and two clapboard buildings boasting tall white pillars with matching trim. Oaks and pines graced the landscape, and birds sung perfect melodies as they glided through the salt air.

A fiftyish gentleman approached us as we exited the car and McGrath sauntered to the trunk to grab his tools. I recognized Ben Carlson from the photograph on the museum website. Of average height, his white hair and beard, welcoming smile, and wire-rimmed glasses made him look a bit like Santa Claus.

Ben's plaid shirt and loose-fitting Levis bespoke wood carver through and through. The glint in his eyes told me of a wisdom I was eager to understand. In any case, he put me immediately at ease, and left me confident McGrath had wound up in the right place at the right time.

"You must be Samantha," he said softly. "Welcome."

As I shook Ben's hand, he folded his hand over mine and held it for a moment. An increased sense of serenity overtook me. I glanced back at McGrath. "This is my friend, Jim McGrath."

He and McGrath shook hands and exchanged pleasantries about the weather and the peaceful surroundings.

I peered down the street. "Is there a library close by?"

"Might have passed it on your way in." Ben pointed down the road with a gnarled index finger, then glanced down at my athletic shoes. "'Bout a quarter mile down the road."

"Perfect," I said. "How long do you two need?"

"Got a cell phone?" Ben asked, checking his watch.

I pulled out my phone.

"It's a beautiful morning. Got some coffee brewing. I want to settle Jim into the surroundings. Give us a couple of hours."

"May I see your studio?" I couldn't help myself. As much as my gut told me Ben was the guy I wanted McGrath to spend time with, my motherly instinct stuck out its ridiculous, protective head.

"Let us carve for a while. Once we've finished, you can check out what we've accomplished and I'll give you the complete tour."

"Do you always work inside? The grounds are spectacular. I'm inspired just standing here."

"Well," he said, chuckling softly. "There is more light out here." His eyes twinkled with insight.

I narrowed my gaze. Just as I'd suspected, this man bore a keen intellect. Teacher, as Helen Keller had called Anne Sullivan, came to mind as his proper title. I wondered what brought a man like him to the boonies—had to be quite a story there.

Accepting my gentle dismissal, I kissed McGrath on the cheek before retrieving my backpack and laptop from the car and traversing the quaint village road. Less than five minutes later, I found myself standing in front of a small cedar-shake cottage-y affair, again with white trim. A simple sign: "Public

Library," was affixed above the heavy wooden door. The library blended into the natural surroundings, as everything on Mt. Desert Island seemed to do. Neat. Tidy. New England through and through.

I entered the space, lined knotty pine ceilings rose above shelves upon shelves of books. Well-worn pages, one of my favorite aphrodisiacs, slowed my pulse to the powered-down level I'd often witnessed in my Lizzie when she parked in front of the television. Wicker chairs were placed throughout, tucked in nooks and crannies. More like a reading room than a typical suburban library. An old oak card catalog, polished to a high gloss, added further charm to the place. The place was full of history, each person who'd entered the doors since its opening had their own stories to tell. I settled into a cushioned corner chair and Googled the library. Silly, I know, but a force pulled me in, like whenever I smelled chlorine. I couldn't resist the urge to dive in and swim.

The building I was sitting in was constructed in 1898. I read all about the woman who'd begun collecting discarded books from summer hotels and placed them on a drug store shelf until the collected works grew enough that she moved them to an old coffin shop. No surprise a woman had the ingenuity to create a library in a small town like this. Friends of the library had gathered donations to build the place I sat in today.

"Thank you," I whispered.

CHAPTER SEVEN

BEFORE I HEADED back to the museum to check in on Ben and his new student, I wandered across the street to a small town coffee shop. Rows of books lined the shelves. The place reminded me of The Daily Grind, the quaint little cafe back home that served as our town's first library. This shop was fashioned in the same way, but with books from local authors, some about local history and events.

Turned out other's were as intrigued by Sir Harry's murder as I. The former owner of our inn had been written about numerous times—suppositions about the unsolved homicide. I gathered seven paperbacks into my arms, paid for them, and stuffed them into my backpack before claiming my coffee and roaming outside to find a park bench where I could begin to read more about Harry, my new addiction.

I sipped my coffee and read. Politics, greed, passion.

When I stopped to glance at my watch, I realized

I'd stayed away too long. Ben had suggested they needed two hours for their first session, and almost three hours had passed. I hefted my backpack onto my shoulders, tossed my cup into a nearby trash bin, and trekked down the street to the museum.

I entered the spotless facility and was met by a cozy brick fireplace with a log mantle. A relief carving of two cormorants, facing each other as if meeting for the first time, was displayed on the rustic timber. On the oversized hearth sat life-size carvings of shorebirds, ones I had seen but couldn't name. The other three walls were adorned with paintings of birds. Owls, eagles, black-capped chickadees, green herons, Great egrets, and a single sandpiper.

Peaceful surroundings, complete quiet. Glass cases protected carvings of pileated woodpeckers, eider ducks, birds in flight. I stood in awe, totally enamored by the work and the plethora of nature I'd never before seen.

I meandered through the museum for a few more minutes, allowing the scent of sawdust and pine to lead me to the back of the building and the murmur of voices. I spotted the men huddled over their work. Ben, with his glasses perched on the tip of his nose, wore a red apron over his plaid shirt. He held a knife and small block of pine in his hands, his touch as gentle as if he were holding an injured fledgling.

The calm manner I had observed at our meeting continued in his hushed voice as he uttered words of encouragement.

"You're a talented guy," he said. "Carving is in your blood. Many carvers need a drawing to work from, but you appear to hold detailed pencil drawings in your head."

I noticed the photograph of a bird, which sat on the wood block table in front of Ben. He seemed to be carving from the photo.

McGrath narrowed his eyes, but didn't look up. His attention remained on his block of wood, taking the shape of a tiny bird. Ben's gaze returned to his hands.

I cleared my throat to signal my arrival. Ben looked up first.

"Samantha," he said. He carefully set his carving on the table, stood, brushed off the front of his apron and offered me his hand.

"It's so quiet in here."

"Sometimes I listen to music while I'm carving," Ben said, "but I didn't want any distractions today." His gaze drifted to McGrath, still intent on his whittling.

"I can wait outside if you two aren't finished."

McGrath's focus remained on his work. His therapy had taken on a life of its own. Just like me and a swimming pool. Once I created a rhythm with my stroke, I could swim for hours.

I winked at Ben and eased out of the room. He followed me and we exited the building.

Ben faced me. "He's quite skilled. And very creative. Of course, I've never seen his previous work, but he's obviously done this before—"

"It does my heart good to see him so immersed in a project," I said, a sudden lump growing in my throat. My eyes filled with tears, though I fought to keep them at bay. "Sorry," I apologized. "It's been a long time since I've witnessed him doing anything that seemed all his."

Ben rested a hand gently on my shoulder. "I don't know any more of his story than what you've told me, but I know from personal experience how healing creative work can be. Give him time. How long has it been since the shooting?"

"Eleven months. He's remembered more since we arrived in Bar Harbor than he has in all those months, but his recollections are mostly work-related. I don't know what to do." A tear snaked down my cheek.

Ben offered his hankie. "Sounds like you've weathered a ton the past year. It's normal to feel a letdown now that you're here and see him making some progress. You can take a breath now, the crisis has lifted."

I blew my nose and tucked his handkerchief in my pocket. "I'll wash this and return it."

Ben tipped his head. "Keep it. I have plenty more."

I stood back and peered at him. This man was a gift. He also had answers. Keys to life. I wanted to lap up every word.

"Would you like to join us for a drink later?" I asked.

"The two of you need time together. Don't rush socializing. I know the temptation, since he's regaining some memories, but try to relax and enjoy each other's company. I can see you two love each other very much."

"Really? How can you tell?"

"You're easy with each other. You're like dancers who've been forever partners—your glances speak volumes. No words necessary."

Weird. He'd only seen us interact for a few moments when I'd dropped McGrath off. "What do you do in your off hours? Read palms?"

Ben chuckled, a soft gravel. "Let's go inside and see if we can crack the magnetic force. I want Jim to take a break from his work before he burns out. Is he a perfectionist?"

I cocked my head and closed one eye. "How'd you guess?"

By the time we wound back to the woodshop, McGrath had tidied up his work area and was just hanging his apron on a hook near the rear door. He ambled over and wrapped his arms around me in a bear hug, planting a kiss on my temple.

"Thanks," he said. "Carving is like medicine for me."

I hesitated for a moment, wondering if I should

ask to see his work. Instinct told me he'd show me when he was ready, and Ben's words "don't rush it," replayed in my head.

McGrath's gaze traveled away from me. He shook Ben's hand, and thanked him.

"Tomorrow?" Ben asked.

McGrath gave him the thumbs up.

"Nine o'clock sharp," Ben said. "I'll have the coffee ready."

As we exited the back door, I heard voices in the front of the museum. McGrath had been fortunate enough to have Ben all to himself that morning before the museum opened. Now, I was lucky enough to have McGrath all to myself for the next twenty-one hours.

CHAPTER EIGHT

MCGRATH CLAIMED THE shower, so I sat in the sunshine and let the breeze whip my hair around my face for a few minutes before tying the untamed tresses back and taking a few moments to call the kids. Nick picked up. "Whatcha up to, Mommy?" he said.

He hadn't called me Mommy in a very long time. Tears welled up and clogged my throat. Why was I so emotional?

"How's my boy?" I asked, wanting to hide my sentimental mood from my son.

"Caught a bundle of perch this morning. Cleaned 'em, fried 'em up on the outside burner. Daddy would be proud of me. I begged Grandpa Ed to let me buy some of the batter mix Dad used to use. Then I kicked everyone out of the kitchen and whipped up a batch of breading, warmed up the oil, and cooked up those little buggers. You should have tasted 'em, Mom. I'm quite the cook."

Shit. More tears. I needed a drink. Or a

distraction. I swallowed.

"How's the guitar coming along?" What made me ask a provocative question, I'll never know. Nick had lost a good deal of fine-motor skill as a result of his accident. Guitar playing, his passion, had suffered the most and served as the only real lingering effect of his head injury and coma. Just like me not to let well enough alone.

"Good actually. I'm practicing patience. My hand still hurts. I can't make my fingers do what I want them to all the time, but if I play in small doses, I can do a bit more each time."

I couldn't believe how mature he sounded. "Great news, kiddo. What's up with your precious siblings?"

"Annie and Marie are hanging out with boys. One of the dudes has a pierced ear, Mom."

"Shame on you, yanking my chain. Want me to come home early and ruin your summer?"

Nick's laugh was wicked. "Here," he said, "talk to Lizzie."

I spoke to the other four kids. Hearing their voices always proved reassuring when we spent time apart. After I ended the call, I relaxed for a long moment. Although a tough stretch had passed since the shooting, McGrath's recovery alongside Nick's, there had also been no real threat to our lives in all that time. I had much to be thankful for.

The racket of McGrath banging drawers brought me inside.

"Lose something?" I called, before heading into the bedroom.

"My memory," he joked. "Can't find my skivvies."

"Your birthday suit is good enough for me," I said. He stood before me in his blessed nakedness. I patted his fanny before opening a small drawer at the top of the dresser and tossing a pair of BVDs his way.

"Feel like hiking?" I asked.

We stopped at the Visitor Center at Acadia and gathered a few trail maps and pamphlets. Next stop, Jordan Pond. We climbed the modest path to the top of the trail, then looped around to settle on some rocks at the edge of the pond. The scenery left me breathless. We held hands and marveled at Bubble Rock. Clouds, like painted wisps of cotton, spotted a pale blue sky, just above the two mountainous bubbles of igneous rock.

"Have you heard about Popovers?" he asked.

That's my guy. Food focused. Thinking about his next meal. "Popovers?" I gazed behind me at the restaurant. Patrons littered the grounds like feeding squirrels. Adirondack chairs were planted in amongst the trees, and redwood tables with opened umbrellas provided shade to the lunch crowd.

"Eggs, milk, flour. A dash of baking soda and salt. Kind of like a cream puff on steroids." His dimples deepened.

Not only had McGrath become my chief cook

and dishwasher, he'd taken a shine to baking, as well. "We're each going to weigh about three hundred pounds before this trip is over."

"Lobster has no calories," he said. His Maine mantra.

"Vacation food has no calories. More like that, isn't it?" I brushed the side of his face with my hand, treasuring the lines of his face. "Let's go then," I agreed.

We planned our next hike while we waited for a table. Just as he'd predicted, warm popovers arrived at our outdoor table within moments of our being seated. We each ordered a glass of wine, delighted that we had a table away from the fray.

I traced the back of McGrath's hand with my finger. I couldn't imagine how he held the ability to see something in his mind, then carve it without a sketch or a plan. "Tell me about this morning."

"Ben's an interesting guy. He's a sage of sorts."

"What do you mean?" I narrowed my eyes, watching as he spent a long moment thinking about what to say.

"He's quiet. So quiet that he makes me think."

"Does he make you uncomfortable?"

"Remember who you're talking to. I'm never uneasy." McGrath puffed out his chest, which made me smile. "It was as if he was allowing me time to settle in. Get my bearings."

I turned toward him so my knee touched his.

"Bearings are good."

McGrath averted his eyes. "I think he wants me to trust myself."

"That's pretty deep," I said, patting his hand. "I'm not used to this from you."

He ignored me. "You told him about the shooting, right?"

"Yes," I admitted. "I told him your memory had drifted from the shock, or when the bullet nicked your brain." I tried to make light of his injury and what I'd shared with Ben. Nervousness, I guess. I hated to think I'd violated his privacy.

"The way I see things, I'm right where I'm supposed to be. I admit, these recent jogs of memories have been—well, for lack of a better word—unsettling."

My attention shifted to full alert. McGrath so seldom let me in on the soul stuff. He was a man of actions, not words. He'd spent the past months keeping busy with tasks, distractions—supporting the kids and me rather than dealing with his own wounds, physical or otherwise.

"In what way?" This was shaky ground. I didn't want to say the wrong thing. Scare him off. Close him up.

"Has my personality changed since the shooting?"

I hemmed and hawed for a moment.

"Has it?" He pressed the subject.

"No," I said. "I'm just thinking. You're the same guy, minus remembering. It's impossible to separate this out. What life boils down to, for all of us, I guess, is that we become our careers in so many ways. Our work shapes how we think about everything, and affects our very nature. For me, I'm always looking to help someone out, to swoop in, ready to rescue. My students have disabilities. They need my support. I tread this fine line of helping, teaching them to do for themselves, encouraging them to become more independent, yet I struggle with this innate desire to make their lives easier.

"I hate that they have to work so hard for every damn little victory. Don't get me wrong, I'm the first one to turn cartwheels when they're successful, but some days, I just want to make it better. In the end I've become too trusting, too ready to believe what's right in front of me, rather than questioning. I hate to admit it, but I've been manipulated more than once. And I don't seem to be able to cure my naiveté.

"I'm not sure if I'm making sense, but I've *become* a teacher. It's who I am, what I do. Nothing will ever change that about me. Twenty-four seven. Whether appropriate or not, I'm a teacher. You, on the other hand, have dealt with the dregs of the earth, so you take nothing at face value. You were always questioning. Always suspicious."

"Are you saying I've changed? I don't question anymore?"

"One of the things that attracted me to you was your analytical mind. But along with it came this anodized-steel exterior. This strong, steady, private presence. It's still there, but I think—whether you're aware of it or not—your confidence suffered with the shooting. Losing your past left you a bit unsteady, is all."

"You still like me though, right? I am an extremely attractive man." He cocked his head, winking like he'd just seen me for the first time and was making a move.

I burst into laughter—knocked the table with my knee and overturned my water glass. Tears streamed down my face. The couple at the next table craned their necks to investigate. I waved my hand, letting them know there was nothing to share or be concerned about as I mopped up the water with my napkin.

"I like you more than ever," I said. "I can't imagine what life is like for you. Not that I spend an inordinate amount of time thinking about my past. Actually, I'm a bit jealous. There are times I'd like a fresh start."

"Fresh start," he repeated. "Not sure what that means."

"Me either," I admitted. "Trust this. You're the same guy you've always been. Your instincts haven't changed. You're still the guy I met and fell in love with. You're smart, intuitive, accomplished. The confidence will return. The knowing. Or at least the understanding of who you are and who you're meant to be."

"I don't know who I am because I can't remember where I've been." He winced. "More than anything, I find this unnerving. 'Un.'Prefix of the day, I guess. I'm undone. I'm not sure who I'm supposed to be, where I'm supposed to be."

"Yet you just said you are where you're supposed to be. Conflicted?"

McGrath's turn to laugh. "Unnerved. Conflicted. All of the above. But the carving felt good. Familiar even."

"Muscle memory."

"A memory that stays intact when all else disappears."

"So, at least with carving comes a certain peace. Let yourself settle in." I paused. "You've just triggered a thought. Raising kids provides me with a purpose. Since I have so many children—between my own and my students—most times I hardly have the time and space to think of anything else. Busy is a blessing when times are tough. I can't get in my head too often, nor can I stay there for a continuous sixty seconds. Maybe your focus on the kids and me has been a plus. But now, we've lifted the craziness. You have time to find you again."

"Scares the shit out of me."

I grinned, but quickly became serious. "You, my

dear, are going to be fine."

We spent the next twenty minutes focusing on our salads and the luscious popovers.

"When you feel conflicted and need to avoid feeling unsettled, you can bake these for me."

"Deal," he said.

CHAPTER NINE

THE WILLOWS AND its accompanying hotel, The Atlantic Oceanside, were short a bar, so we settled in at the Jack Russell across the street, since we could walk home if we were over-served. Another converted down-east home, cedar-shaked and full of charm, the curved oak bar welcomed visitors. Twinkle lights adorned the entryway and windows, and tall oak chairs were poised at a sit-yourself-down angle. Adam, our young bartender, held all the local flavor of the Island. A spunky, eccentric guy with spiked hair, his passion for the beverages he concocted held our attention for a good two hours. As tempted as I was to pump him for information about the Sir Harry Oakes mystery, I didn't want to let McGrath in on what I'd busied myself with while he'd been carving with Ben. He might think I was crazy and race up Cadillac Mountain and hide.

Instead, we focused on the newest addition to the cocktail list—blueberry-infused vodka with blueberry ice cubes—a drink Adam had dreamt up, but was, as yet, unnamed. After McGrath and I had each finished a glass of wine, Adam implored us to be guinea pigs for his concoction. He pressed a muddle of lime and fresh mint into a tall glass, poured in a shot of the blueberry vodka, a touch of St. Germaine (the liqueur created from freshly picked elderflower blossoms in the French Alps, which held an enormous magical appeal for me) a splash of soda, and floated one of his homemade blueberry ice cubes on top, with a sprig of mint.

Blueberry Passion. Blue Moon. Berry Blue. Something Blue.

Maybe by the end of vacation, we'd find a name. In the meantime, I crowned the delicacy "delicious."

By the following morning, McGrath and I had settled into a routine. A run first thing, then showers and lousy hotel coffee while we dressed and prepared for our day. We left for Southwest Harbor a little earlier this time, motivated by the appeal of a real cup of coffee from the shop across from the local library.

At the museum, we spent a few minutes wandering the grounds. Not too far off in the distance, in a quiet stand of trees on the edge of the woods, we spotted Ben. His slow movement or poses resembled a form of meditation, like yoga, but not quite. I'd taken a yoga class once and loved stretching, just never found the time to fit the practice into my schedule on a permanent basis.

McGrath and I turned and strode back towards

the museum, not wanting to disturb Ben, and waited on a park bench near the museum's entrance.

"I'm intrigued by him," I said.

McGrath nodded.

"What do you think his story is?"

"Good question," McGrath agreed. "Ideas?"

"He's mysterious. I'm guessing not very easy to know. I don't know him well enough yet to make a reasonable guess, but if I had to say, I'd venture he's more comfortable immersing himself in other people's lives than sharing his own."

"You're pretty good at sizing people up," McGrath said. "I've watched you. Funny, but you said yesterday that you consider yourself naïve, how you accept people at face value and believe they are at their best, but I've also seen you shoot to the heart of the matter when the kids are trying to avoid a subject. Remember the night I first came to the house? Annie was furious. She wanted nothing to do with me. You saw right through her and recognized that she was struggling because you were introducing a new man into her life."

He remembered.

"Annie struggles with transitions. She's been through lots of loss in her life. New situations raise all kinds of trust issues for her. I try to ease her into things, let her kick and scream, as it were. Eventually, she comes around." I laughed as I remembered. "Trust me, when Jon entered our lives, the two of them were like boxers in a ring. A test period of several months passed before she settled in. Then, the two of them were as inseparable as salt and pepper. In the end, they came to complement each other exquisitely."

"So," McGrath said, "take a guess about Ben."

"I'd say he's been through some heavy shit in his life. He's learned from the pain, but isn't willing to share his past, so he inserts himself—in his own quiet, ever-present way—into other's lives, realizing that listening is healing, and just being there is therapeutic."

"See," McGrath said, "You do know."

"Remains to be seen." I pointed over McGrath's head. "He's coming."

Ben joined us at the bench. "Good morning," he said. "Good to see you both."

"We didn't mean to spy or intrude on your exercise," I apologized.

"Parting the wild horse's mane," Ben said. "My morning ritual."

"A form of meditation?" I asked.

"So much more," Ben said simply before locking eyes with McGrath. "Let's get carving. I put some coffee on before I hit the woods. Should be ready."

I stood and shook Ben's hand. "I'll entrust him to you."

Ben glanced at his student with a sly smile. "She's a mother at heart, isn't she?"

McGrath just smiled and nodded. He kissed me on the cheek before following Ben inside.

"Have fun!" I called out, and strode down the street to the library. There were many possible next steps in my research of Sir Harry's death. I could read one of the books about his death and trial, but that would be like putting a bookcase together without reading the instructions, a practice men were often guilty of—women, not so much.

I scrunched my brows at my not-so-solid logic. In truth, I put impulsivity at the top of my personal weaknesses list. At least for today, I reasoned, I'd pursue this investigation in chronological order.

I inhaled the smell of weathered pages as I entered the library. All those stories. I wished I could simply breathe them in and they'd become part of me. Creature of habit that I am, I peered around the corner and checked out the chair I had occupied yesterday. To my relief, the spot was empty, waiting for me. I propped my computer on a nearby table, grabbed one of the books I'd purchased from the coffee shop, and spent the next two hours getting to know Harry a little better.

Oakes was a tough guy. He'd spent time chipping rock in frigid temperatures, up to sixty degrees below zero, in the Yukon. At one point in 1906, he became shipwrecked off the coast of Alaska and wound up being taken prisoner by the Russians for a short time before being released. His endless search for gold took him to Australia, New Zealand, and California, where he nearly died of heatstroke. I developed this picture of him. Short. Stocky. Determined. More than a little obsessed.

He arrived in Ontario, Canada, in 1911. By then he would have been thirty-eight years old. He'd spent the bulk of his adult life searching for gold. Had I been him, I would have given up a long time ago—right after the first frostbite incident. He'd had to have been a little crazy to continue this pursuit after so much disappointment.

But as I read more, I could see the tables were about to turn for my friend Harry. He met a woman named Roza Brown. She owned the rooming house in which Henry had decided to board, and while she despised the miners she rented to, she took a shining to Harry. In fact, Roza put him on the trail to Kirkland Lake and his ultimate gold strike. Since Harry had run out of money by that time, he set out to secure some partners. The Tough brothers, all four of them, joined Harry in staking claims on a mine. They trudged in 52 degree below zero weather, after midnight, through a snowfall—for seven miles. After driving their stakes, they toasted the Tough-Oakes claim.

They made some money, but, as a partnership often does, their alliance fell apart. Harry sold off his claim, and with the money he'd made, set about to make another. In 1918, the laughing stock of many,

Harry made a bold decision. He decided to mine beneath Kirkland Lake, thanks to the financial support of his mother. Harry's cockamamie idea paid off when he discovered more gold than he could have ever hoped for. The Oakes'Lake Shore mine at Kirkland Lake became one of the largest producers of gold in the Western Hemisphere. By the 1920s, Harry was pulling in $60,000 a day.

I applauded Harry. His courage and tenacity were admirable, but already knowing the end to the story made me sad. He'd been murdered about twenty years later.

I speculated then. Maybe he was a shyster. Maybe his wealth provided a motivation for his killing. Maybe he was a lousy alcoholic, or a player. Crimes of passion where the most common crimes, after all.

My mind wandered to my husband's impostor, Jon Stitsill. I'd never been able to understand his motivation for committing the number of assassinations he'd notched on his belt. Money, sure. But what had that money afforded him? As far as I could tell, even though he'd certainly achieved a certain level of wealth, he hadn't bought a nice home, vacationed wildly, ever had a wife or family he was happy about. I decided a long time ago he was a sick individual, never looking past the immediate future, just doing what he needed to do to accomplish his next goal—which seemed only to be eradicating others—and complete the next job without getting caught. Pure evil. That's who he was.

My head began to throb. Too much to sort out. I turned my attention back to my book and read on.

When Oakes struck gold, he became the wealthiest man in Canada. An affluent fellow who shared his good fortune with others, Harry lived a life of luxury, building himself a chateau and a golf course with splendid views of the lake, but only after sending money to his family, all those who had believed in him and shared what little they could afford. His generosity made them richer than they ever could have imagined.

"Why would someone want to kill him?" I muttered to myself.

A self-proclaimed "restless man," Harry needed something to keep his attention, even after attaining his goal. He set sail on a world cruise and met Eunice McIntyre, an Australian lady twenty-six years his junior, and they married after a whirlwind romance. At the ripe old age of forty-nine, Sir Harry married for the first time. Eunice had been six inches taller than Harry. She was a way better woman than me—I needed a taller man. Perhaps Harry's millionaire status influenced her decision.

In any case, they returned to Kirkland for a short time before settling in Niagara Falls. Here, they had five children. Just like me. Nancy, born in 1924, Sydney, three years later, in 1927. Then Shirley,

William, and Harry, in 1929, 1930, and 1932. Five kids in eight years. Eunice had to have been as crazy as me. For sure.

When Harry Jr. turned two years of age, in 1934, the Oakes family moved to the Bahamas for tax reasons. They summered in Bar Harbor, at The Willows. Finally, I was up to speed. So, the Bahamas was their permanent residence, and The Willows was their summer home.

I pulled my computer onto my lap and Googled "Eunice Oakes." Drawn to her image—a beautiful young woman with clear brown eyes, thick wavy hair, and a delicately dimpled chin—I tried to see inside her, imagine what she was like. Photographs of her and her family seemed relaxed, as if she were a mom delighting in her children, gathered around Harry and her like blooms on a rosebush. In one particular photo, she gazed at Harry, who was gleaming with pride, holding his youngest in his lap. Interestingly enough, she seemed rather down to earth. A young mother devoted to her children.

Old filmstrips were posted on You Tube, and I spent even more time viewing them. I must be out of my mind, spending so many hours with these dead folks. Disgusted with my silly preoccupation with Harry's life and death, I packed up my computer, nodded goodbye to the gray-haired librarian behind her desk, and marched across the street to the coffee shop.

But, I proved as tenacious as Harry, for the "greatest unsolved murder mystery of all time," or so I'd read, had gripped its tentacles around my brain, and they refused to unleash their hold.

I ordered a fat-free, skim vanilla latte, then settled in with my laptop at a tiny carved table in the rear of the shop to research Harry's children. Find a link. Nancy first, I thought. The oldest and the wife of the man accused in her father's death, it made the most sense to start there.

I was in the thick of the story now. Nancy had quite a life. Harry had been murdered the night before he was to travel to The Willows to vacation with Eunice and their five children, on July 8, 1943. His friend, Harold Christie, who had spent the night at Harry's home, discovered his body. When Harold went looking for his friend that morning, he found Harry still in bed, his body partially destroyed by fire. His murderer had attempted to cover up the killing by dousing Harry in gasoline, covering his body with pillows and feathers, and setting a fan bedside to fuel the flames. A thunderstorm thwarted the efforts to blanket the crime, the torrential rain extinguishing the house fire. An autopsy concluded that Harry had suffered a broken skull when beat about the head with a blunt instrument.

The further I read, the stickier the situation became. The Duke of Windsor involved himself, insisting on bringing in two Miami detectives to conduct the murder investigation. From what I read, the guys resembled Abbot and Costello, botching the scene, leaving their evidence equipment stateside, and forgetting, by the time the accuser went to trial, crucial timetables. Nancy's husband was charged with the crime. Alfred de Marigny, a heartthrob and playboy, had married Nancy three days after she turned nineteen. A fortune-seeker himself, he appeared to seize the opportunity for easy wealth. He and Harry hated each other. Seemed like a slam-dunk.

But Alfred had been acquitted two hours after the jury had gone into deliberations, no doubt, I guessed, because of the substandard investigation. The case was never reopened. Never solved.

Now my real work began. I had volumes of information to tread through, but a quick glance at the clock told me time was up. I had to head down the street and meet up with McGrath.

CHAPTER TEN

A S I WANDERED down the street, avoiding cracks in the sidewalk as I'd done as a child, I twisted ideas. I could pursue Harry's kids' lives, or his widow's life, or the acquitted son-in-law, Alfred DeMarigny.

I entered the museum before I had the chance to make a definitive decision, and quietly passed through the display rooms to the workshop at the rear of the museum. I paused in the doorway, like a thespian, and swallowed the scene whole. A goggle-eyed Ben, bent over his round of pine, etched fine lines into the soft wood, while McGrath, eyes narrowed to slits, studied a section of a bird's wing, no doubt deciding whether more definition was needed as his fish tail gouge (I'd studied the tool names) remained poised in his hand.

When McGrath spoke, I, seasoned eavesdropper of adolescents, ducked back a bit to a vantage point from which I could spy, and strained to hear.

"She's a tough lady. Lost her husband a couple of

years ago in an auto accident while he was on business in Japan. Sounds like he'd been traveling for business since they'd married, so she was already raising their five kids pretty much single-handedly while holding down a full-time teaching position. After his death, she adopted his two kids, and has been bringing them up ever since."

"That explains the momma bear attitude," Ben said, nodding.

"She's sweet, smart, and sassy." A smile crossed McGrath's face. "The gods shined on me when they brought her into my life. I don't know how I would have gotten through these past months without her. Guess she's used to picking up strays."

"Don't kid yourself," Ben said. "I'm sure you bring plenty to the party."

"Not too sure about that. An unemployed cop. Disabled even."

"Temporarily." Ben shot a finger at McGrath's work. "Let me see," he added.

McGrath held up his carving. Clearly a bird, but the breed indecipherable to me, I marveled at the quality of his work. I don't have the patience for slow, tedious work.

"You're a natural. Already, I can see improvement in your lines. Not everyone can commit a Baltimore Oriole to memory."

McGrath's shoulders squared. He took a long breath and let it out slowly. I used the opportunity, the lull in conversation, to enter the room, but stood just inside the doorway, not wanting to disturb them.

Ben lifted his goggles to the top of his forehead and rested them there. A second later, he wound around on his stool, spotted me and smiled, his head tipping forward to McGrath's carving momentarily, then back to me. He arched his eyebrows in approval.

"He's quite the artist, right, Samantha?"

"I've always thought so." I returned Ben's smile.

"Before long," Ben added, "your friend here will have an exhibit devoted to his work. You should spend the summer. Detective McGrath can assume the role of guest carver for the season. He's skilled enough to teach classes. In fact, I'd like to suggest he consider spending an afternoon or two here each week, to work with some of our local talent."

McGrath blushed. I recognized the idea held immediate appeal, but he hesitated to speak.

"Think about it," Ben said as he walked behind McGrath and rested a heavy, convincing palm on his shoulder. "There's a place for you here."

An entire summer in Maine. Certainly not what we'd planned, but not an impossible proposition. I'd call Ed and discuss the possibility. Even if we stretched our visit to three or four weeks, we couldn't spend the time better. McGrath's confidence was slowly seeping back. In my mind, the more time spent in Bar Harbor, the better.

McGrath eased up from his stool, stretching out

his cramped back and shoulders, reaching up high over his head to ease out the kinks. Then, he began to clean up his mess, after delivering his work-in-progress to a nearby shelf, which already bore his name. I beamed, proud as the first day of Kindergarten with Lizzie, watching her deposit her backpack in her cubby. Her home away from home. McGrath's path back.

We said our goodbyes, telling Ben we'd see him the next morning, and headed out into the midday sunshine. "Feel like a walk?"

McGrath laced his fingers in mine and swung our arms, a pendulum keeping time. "Beautiful day," he said.

I glanced at his profile. Before my very eyes, he was coming back to me. Confident, happy, whole again. A chill shot down my spine. If I'd known whittling wood was the ticket, I would have put a block of pine in his hands months ago.

"Let's grab a cup of coffee and head to the beach."

McGrath kissed me. "Thanks," he said.

I swung my head around so he couldn't see my tears.

We strolled into the quaint little shop and McGrath approached the counter. He ordered us each a tall black coffee and went about finding cup sleeves and napkins while I parked by the bookshelf and turned pages on yet another Sir Harry Oakes publication. This one held more photos. Intrigued, I rifled inside my purse for my wallet.

McGrath came up behind me, peering over my shoulder. "What have we here?" he asked as he planted a kiss on my neck.

"I'm being silly," I said. "I'm intrigued with the Harry Oakes murder. Don't ask me why, but I love true crime."

"Not enough of that in your own life?" McGrath joked.

"Life's been quiet for a while, you know?"

"Trouble magnet," McGrath teased. "You're downright dangerous."

"You're right. I'm weird. But my obsession is keeping me off the streets while you're carving."

McGrath plucked the book from my hands. "My gift to you, then."

After he paid for the book, tucking the hardback under his arm, we meandered down the street to the beach. I found a perch within a cropping of rocks and sat down. McGrath settled in beside me, set his coffee down, knees bent up toward his chest, and began to page through the book.

I pointed out Harry, his wife, Eunice, and the children, all the while filling him in on Harry's early life, his personality, and his success.

"You've really gotten to know this guy."

I shrugged, a bit embarrassed. "This is true."

"Don't worry. I don't think you're crazy. I'm a

cop, remember? Cold cases get to me, too."

"We'd be heroes if we figured this one out. He died in 1943. In the Bahamas."

"Pretty darned cold."

"We'd be like superheroes, doing what no man had done before."

"Next summer's trip," he suggested.

I became quiet. Pensive.

"Too long for you to wait?"

"Afraid so."

"Tell you what," McGrath said. "If you find anything local, a path we can pursue, we'll work on solving this mystery in the afternoons once I'm done carving. Deal?"

I lit up like the twinkle lights on a Christmas tree. "Deal."

I sipped my coffee, gazed out at the sea, and felt blessed. This man loved me enough to put up with my crazy ideas. My obsessions even. I kissed him on the cheek. "Too bad these boulders aren't more comfy. I'd tackle you right here."

McGrath wrapped a hand around each eye, forming a set of imaginary binoculars. He combed the area. "Not another soul in sight," he said. "Let's get creative."

CHAPTER ELEVEN

BACK AT THE hotel after a quick shower, I sat on the deck and waited for McGrath to finish gussying up. I leafed through the pages of the book, peering over the family photos and the Oakes'Bahamas home. I settled on a snapshot of Alfred de Marigny, goose bumps peppering my arms. He looked familiar. Strikingly so.

I read his bio. The man died in 1998 in Houston, Texas. He and Nancy had divorced in the mid 50s. I did the math. He would have been about 45 years old at the time of their divorce. Plenty of time for more chapters in his life.

I can't say why, but I shut the book when I heard footsteps. There was something about Alfred. I needed time to think and pull the pieces together. I couldn't possibly know a dead guy who lived in another part of the country, one I'd never visited.

"What's up?" McGrath asked. "You look distracted—disturbed even."

"Feeling unsettled. I can't say why." I rubbed my

arms.

"I'd have thought my creative love-making techniques would have prevented anxiety for a lot longer than an hour or so."

"Sorry," I said, forcing a smile. "I'm deranged, is all. What's next on the agenda?"

"Let's hike across the land bridge."

I laced up my tennies and we strolled in to town, discovering the path leading from the harbor to Bar Island. The trail across was usually covered with water so deep that lobster boats could motor across. I tried to distract myself with the glorious views, the dappled deer camouflaged in the deep woods, and the aroma of the pines, but no luck.

In my mind's eye, I saw the face of Alfred de Marigny, or Freddie, as I'd affectionately dubbed him. I swallowed hard, focusing on his face. Something about his eyes. I envisioned his body, the breadth of his shoulders, the length of his arms. His long arms. Just like Jon's impostor. I shook my head, hoping to relieve myself of this ridiculous notion. No way could there be a connection.

I retraced my memory of the photograph. A remarkable resemblance existed. Freddie had lived in Canada for a while after his divorce from Nancy. In 1962, he could have fathered a son. I did the math. Freddie had been born in 1910. He would have been 52 at the time of the impostor's birth. The timing worked. It also made a great deal of sense that his son would have wound up becoming the same type of scum ball as his dad. Apple. Tree.

My heart skipped several beats, but I couldn't ruin our sightseeing with my sudden urge to get back to my book and my laptop. My research would have to wait until tomorrow morning while McGrath was carving. I warned myself not to get too wrapped up in this mystery. Cautioned myself not to become carried away with schoolgirl suppositions. I'd never been good at letting things rest though. Damned impulsive woman that I am.

I desperately needed a cigarette. Too bad I didn't smoke.

***

Somehow I managed to sleep a few hours. McGrath had no idea that I'd lost my mind. I dropped him off at the museum, trotted down the street to the library, and powered up my laptop. I Googled photos of Freddie, mentally slapping myself for having burned Stitsill's photos in the fire, along with all the fake passports. Would I never learn? There could have been a plethora of clues there. I'd never toss anything again. Scan and save would become my new approach to managing my life.

But I could Google Stitsill. Surely, there had to be a photograph of him somewhere on the web. I searched his chosen name for the time he'd been at the

Japanese Embassy. Nathan Drummond. No photos. Impossible. Then again, he was the master of deception. He would have made sure his face stayed out of the limelight. Shit.

Still, I'd locked eyes with the man once, and the terror had never left me. I stared at the photograph of Alfred de Marigny. The likeness was undeniable. These guys had to be related.

I needed coffee. Strong and black. I packed up my laptop and hurried across the street. Short of traveling to Canada and tracking down the Marigny clan, I couldn't think of another tack that made sense. Unless the family lived close to Maine, the idea was ridiculous. After purchasing a tall mug of French roast, I wandered to a table near the back of the shop, hoping for some privacy—and the strike of a lightning bolt. There had to be an easier way.

I sipped my coffee, took a deep breath, and sat back in my chair. *Leave well enough alone, Samantha. The guy's dead. Your life is calming down, coming together. Joey and Emilio have a happy home with Di. If you look into Stitsill's family, and have the good fortune to find his grown children, then you have to share with them that they have siblings. But wouldn't they know that already?*

Stop. Breathe.

I looked up for a moment and caught the eye of a middle-aged woman, trim in her matching exercise gear. Stunning, in fact, with the deepest, bluest eyes

I'd ever seen and a runner's body, she offered a friendly grin, then took a seat at the table next to mine.

"Hi," she said. "Are you visiting?"

"Am I that obvious?"

"My name's Katharine. Katharine Nelson." She offered me her hand.

"Samantha Stitsill," I said.

"I didn't mean to interrupt, but I've noticed you the past few days, stopping off at the museum and then heading to the library. I haven't seen you around before, so …"

"You must be a local then."

"Lived here all my life."

I took a long moment to assess the woman. The smile lines around her eyes gave away her age, probably fifty, but she was in such great shape, she could have passed for much younger. Her eyes were almost violet and seemed to deepen as she spoke. Her hair, chocolate brown, was skimmed back into a ponytail. She looked strong and well muscled, but fresh, as if her run was still ahead of her.

I glanced down at her hand. No wedding ring. Then again, I never wore my rings when I was out for a run. "It's a beautiful place."

"Are you a carver?" she asked.

I chuckled. "I wish," I said. "My friend is, and he's spending time with the master carver this week."

"Ben? How is he?"

I tried to hide my confusion. If Katharine had lived here her entire life, wouldn't she see Ben regularly? The town, postage-stamp small, would lend itself to common crossings of residents.

"He seems fine. I can't say I know him well enough to answer you, though. He's an interesting guy, for sure."

"What do you mean?" Katharine asked.

"He's an old soul. Wise. I can't quite put my finger on it, but my guess is he's endured a lot in his life." Why I was sharing with this woman I couldn't say. She seemed safe, open. A friend.

"He's been through a lot," she said, a faraway look replacing her smile.

I waited a long moment for her to say more, but she didn't.

"Well," I said. "He seems like a nice guy, and his talent is obvious."

"What do you do?"

"I'm a special education consultant. I spend my days teaching middle schoolers. Then, I have my own five kids too."

"Five children. I can't imagine." She glanced at my hand.

"A widow," I offered.

"I'm so sorry," she said.

I swallowed over the lump in my throat. I'd been widowed almost two years now, but I rarely said the word aloud. Seldom let my marital status define me.

The room turned upside down and I grasped the edge of the table, waiting a prolonged second for the room to stop spinning.

"Two years now," I said, trying to will the chill from my arms. "What about you? Are you married?"

"I am. He's a great guy." She sounded as if she were trying to convince herself.

"Children?" I asked, standing to refill my mug.

"No. I lost a baby years ago. Never had the heart to put myself through a pregnancy again."

"Now it's my turn to be sorry."

We went quiet for a long moment. Finally, I broke the silence.

"Are you a runner?"

Katharine seemed startled out of some deep trance. "Oh, yes." She glimpsed down at her clothes and running shoes. "In fact, I was headed to the beach before I came into the shop. For some reason, coffee sounded better than a run."

"I avoid running like the plague. I have a friend back home who speed walks with me. Occasionally, I run by myself, but not so much anymore." My heart longed for my dog, Rex, and our five-milers, and a sharp pang hit my chest dead center. "Are you a marathoner?"

"Definitely not. Don't have the stomach for the training. I usually run three to five miles a day."

I checked my watch. Plenty of time before I had to head back to the museum. "I'm in town for the next week or so. If you ever want a running partner, I'd be happy to join you. I think I can make three miles at least."

"Sounds great. Want to meet tomorrow morning? Say 9:30?"

Running with a new buddy did sound great, and Lord knows, I needed a distraction. "It's a date."

Katharine shook my hand, mentioned that I should say hello to Ben for her, stood, placed her empty cup in the trash, and left. I watched as she jogged past the plate glass window at the front of the shop, then sauntered back to the museum, tucked my laptop and backpack in the trunk, and went for an unhurried stroll.

I had a lot to think about.

By the time I got back at the museum, the temperature had risen to the mid-seventies and the gentle offshore breeze made the day sublime. Breathing in the beauty and magnificence of my surroundings distracted me. I decided to call Ed and the kids and check the temperature for extending our stay in Maine.

A bench tucked in among the pine trees seemed like the perfect spot to sit while I made the call. I dialed and said a small prayer that one of the kids would pick up. On a day like this, I'd be hard pressed to find someone indoors. On the seventh ring, Lizzie picked up.

"Mommy! Hi!"

A lump formed in my throat for the second time today. I missed my kids with all my heart and yearned for the day when I'd spend the summers with them, rather than away from them. My cockamamie life needed simplification.

"I miss you, sweetie," I said. "Are you having fun?"

"We're having a blast. Grandpa Ed and Grandma Helen do everything for us. Not that you don't, Mom, but we hardly have any chores at all."

"Great. They're spoiling you. You'll be a wretched group by the time I get back home."

Lizzie giggled. "We'll be all right. Don't worry."

"Just warn your siblings for me, okay? Easy street is not what I had in mind for any of you."

"Want to talk to Grandpa?" Lizzie asked, after she filled me in on her latest escapades.

"Sure," I said. "Put him on."

Ed asked about McGrath, and I happily shared the news. "He's remembering, Dad. I can't tell you how relieved I am. His confidence is returning. He's happy and contented in a way I haven't seen in a very long time."

"What a blessing," Ed said.

"Indeed," I answered. "Which brings me to a question. He's been asked to stay the summer—be an artist in residence. I'd like to stay with him, but I'm torn. I don't want to saddle you with the kids, nor do I want to spend the summer away from them."

"Stop. You're a worrywart. Helen and I are having a great time with them. They're amazing kids. Not too many knock-down-drag-outs, either," he joked. "In truth, this is my way of staying close to Jon, Sam. I need this time with them as much as you need and deserve some time away. Now, relax and have a good time."

"What about Nick?" I asked.

"Better every day. The young girls on the beach provide him with plenty of incentive to play guitar. They all enjoy gathering around a good campfire in the evening. I'd say Nick is coming into his own with the ladies."

"Wonderful. Maybe I do need to head home soon."

"I've got the teens under control. I make sure all evening activities are held at our place, so I can keep an eye on them."

"You've always had their numbers."

"Old school," Ed said.

"We are in total agreement."

"It's settled then. I'll break the news to the kids. They'll be heartbroken they have to spend the summer at the beach with their friends."

"I love you, Dad."

"Back at you, young lady."

I ended the call just as Ben and McGrath stepped onto the grounds. I lit up, proud and excited to share my news.

"Here's the lovely Samantha," Ben announced as they approached me.

"Oh, Ben, before I forget, I ran into an old friend of yours. Katharine something. I'm afraid I didn't get her last name."

A sudden pain crossed Ben's face, as if I'd struck him with an arrow. "Katharine Nelson," he said, nodding and avoiding my gaze. Something was definitely up between those two. I made a mental note to pursue the topic with Katharine on our scheduled run tomorrow. With caution.

After Ben abruptly excused himself, McGrath planted a happy kiss on my lips.

"Good morning?" I asked.

He took my hand and traced my fingers with his. "The best."

"I have news."

We drove to an Irish Pub named Paddy's back in Bar Harbor. By the time we arrived some twenty-five minutes later, McGrath had been filled in and I was famished enough to order a beer and a burger with the works, eating a good half of my sandwich before I came up for air.

"Really? Are you okay being away? I don't want to keep you from the kids."

McGrath's smile lines spoke volumes. Clearly, the news delighted him, but good man he was, laid his own life aside for mine.

"I'm a tad conflicted. But in my heart I know the

kids are having a great time. If I were them, I wouldn't want to come home and spend a boring summer with me, doing chores and trying to find friends to hang with. It's summer. Everyone's gone. They might as well stay Up North and have fun." I hesitated for a long moment. "There's something else, too."

McGrath frowned. "What? What's wrong?"

I switched gears and checked my impulsivity. I'd tell him about my suspicions about Stitsill and Marigny another time. "I have to figure out what's gone on with Ben and my new friend, Katharine."

McGrath's scowl changed to a look of puzzlement.

I spent the next thirty minutes playing guessing games with him about their relationship. There was no denying the fact—gossip provided a great distraction.

CHAPTER TWELVE

K YLE ARRIVED IN Lexington a bit after noon, and perused Samantha's street with a quick drive-by before deciding to pull up the long, winding driveway and park. Life was quiet in the country and Samantha's neighborhood fit the rural living code. He assumed the residents were all summering at cottages "Up North," a common occurrence for Michiganders.

Kyle scrutinized the back of the house and took note of the dense woods at the rear of the property, the large pond ringed by huge hosta, and the tree house up in a tall oak before sauntering to the front door.

He wondered if his dad had ever been here. Something—a feeling, a presence— told him he had. Weird and unexplainable, but Kyle had learned long ago to trust his instincts. They'd kept him alive this long, and he wouldn't dismiss them now. He flexed his muscled arms.

"I won't disappoint you, Dad."

Kyle marched to the front door and rang the bell.

He had studied the image of Samantha's face while he drove, setting her photo on the passenger seat and picking her apart. He'd found her picture on the website for the school where she taught. Obviously, a school photo, head shot only, which he found disappointing. He was desperate to know her build, every single thing about her.

Hers was a kind, friendly face, exactly what you'd expect from an elementary school teacher—a half-moon smile, freckled cheeks, knowing eyes, a hint of wisdom, and maybe a tad of mischievousness. In any case, he recognized her intelligence. And if she'd had the cunning to lure her father in, she was a serious contender.

He'd waited long enough. No one was home. Kyle glanced over his shoulder. The street remained empty, so he spent a few minutes peering through the windows. Kids lived here, evidenced by the basketball on the living room floor, and the pair of socks on the floor next to them. Either Samantha wasn't much of a housekeeper or the family had left town in a hurry.

He strolled to the rear of the house, shielding his eyes with his hands so he could see inside the family room window. He nodded with satisfaction. On a table behind the sofa, he spotted framed photographs.

Samantha was fertile. Five kids in all, ranging from about ten years old to mid-teens, if he could count on the photos to be recent, which he told himself he could. A teacher would be sure to display the most recent school photos of her children. Even if she was disorganized enough to let her children leave their clothing and toys strewn across the front room.

The rest of the house seemed tidy enough. So, either they had gone out for a bit, or they were gone for the summer. A bit hard to guess, but he could easily answer the question by hanging around for a few days.

If the family hadn't shown up by midnight tomorrow, he'd go inside and check things out for himself.

Up close and personal.

CHAPTER THIRTEEN

MCGRATH AND I arrived at the museum a few minutes early. I double-checked my shoelaces and attempted to quiet my jitters, shaking out my arms and stretching. Why I'd agreed to run with a complete stranger, I'd never know. Hopefully, I could keep up with her. Youth, don't let me down.

"You're funny," McGrath said, shaking his head.

"How so?" I narrowed my eyes at him.

"You're such a perfectionist. You worry about everything. Just go and have fun."

I tugged down the brim of my cap.

He patted my tush. "You're gonna be fine."

I closed my eyes. "Right."

"Grill her. Get the dirt on her and Ben. Good practice for our next case."

The thought of McGrath and I working another case together excited me. Not the danger part, but the solving-the-mystery part. I gave his cheek a quick peck and trotted down the street, warming up. McGrath was the one coaching me this morning for a change. We were finally headed back to normal. Whatever that was.

I wondered about a trek to Quebec City. And how I'd manage to convince McGrath I should go. Without him.

Simplify, Samantha. One thing at a time.

Katharine sat on the bench outside the shop, adjusting her Garmin. She stood, wrapped her arms around me, then held me at arm's length, a sparkle in her eyes.

"My new running buddy," she said.

All my fears floated away. The sky looked bluer, the breeze welcoming.

"Ready?" she asked.

We took off, setting an easy pace to suit us both.

"Must be great to have lived here your entire life," I said as I took in my surroundings. Stimulated by the fresh air and the promise of a new friend, I picked up speed.

Katharine cast me a sideways glance. "I've lived in a cave." She chuckled casually. "Like I haven't lived at all." She scanned the landscape as if taking in the scenery for the first time. "Funny how we take things for granted."

"I know what you mean about living underground and not noticing the beauty around us. I've lived in the same place my whole life, too. I always feel intimidated by world travelers. They know a helluva lot more than I do."

"Look at us." Katharine pointed back and forth between us. "Two peas in a pod."

I wanted to rush into things right then and there. Ask her how she and Ben knew each other, to divulge their past relationship, how they wound up apart instead of together. Don't ask me how I knew, but my gut told me they should have been an item. Still. I fought off the instinct and did something I seldom do. I began to talk about myself.

"My parents died when I was twenty-two. I have two younger brothers, so I began my teaching career with two siblings in my care. We were like graduated kitchen canisters. Tom was twenty at the time. Mark, twenty-one. I didn't make the best mother substitute."

"Sounds like you grew up together. Plus, I'm guessing you were all grieving at the same time. Makes sense to me that you felt inadequate."

"Mark's a musician." I glanced at her. "Something tells me you'd like him. He's an introvert of sorts, married to his guitar. I worry about him. Tom, too. Neither one of them ever settled down or raised a family."

"So, you're fretting about them while you're raising your own five kids. Sounds like a full plate."

"Enough about me," I said. "What do you do?"

"We have more in common than you might think," she admitted. "I'm a school psychologist."

I did a double-take. I'd missed this. Completely.

"Do you do mostly testing or do you actually

have time to help kids?"

"I do a fair amount of testing, but every now and then I find a few moments to make a difference. I actually began a before-and-after school program to mentor kids whose home life is lacking. We eat breakfast, play games or finish up homework, if need be. I have the chance to feel like I'm doing something worthwhile, rather than spending my life in the diagnostics pool. Only a special ed teacher would understand."

"Trust me, I do."

We headed down a path along the harbor. The gentle slap of waves served as background music and lobster boats wound their way through traps while collecting their catch. I wanted to tell Katharine I really liked her, but I was self-conscious.

"You and Ben. What's that about?"

"Pretty transparent, aren't I?"

"I have the advantage of seeing both you and Ben. When I mentioned your message, he seemed just as unnerved as you did when his name came up."

Katharine grabbed my arm and stopped running. "You talked to him about me?"

We settled into a stroll.

"I just mentioned you said, 'hi.' That's all. But he immediately looked pained. Not like I'm psychic—a casual observer would have noticed his reaction."

"He looked…pained?" Katharine struggled for air.

"Do you want to take a break?" I led her to a park bench that faced the water. "Here. Sit."

"We haven't seen or spoken to each other in years." Tears glimmered in her eyes.

I mentally stepped back. Wispy clouds hung in the blue sky, soft waves rustled along the shore. It was like I was playing a part in a dramatic movie scene.

"How many?"

"We talked on the phone every six months or so until about five years ago."

"Why'd you stop?"

"Too painful."

The tears welled and I passed her a tissue and patted her arm. "I see."

We stayed quiet for a long moment. Katharine finally blew her nose. "Thanks. I haven't talked about him to anyone in years. I guess my feelings were closer to the surface than I expected."

"Jim and I are extending our stay. If you'd like, we can run whenever he spends time with Ben, and if you ever get the urge to talk, I'm a seasoned listener."

"Thanks," she said, getting up. "Let's finish, huh?"

I hated waiting for information.

After our run, we slipped inside the shop for a cool drink, assuming a spot at the rear table where I'd sat yesterday. I toweled off with a napkin before sitting down. "How far did we go?"

Katharine checked her Garmin. "7.2 miles."

"I'm impressed. It's been a long time since I've run."

"Any special reason?"

"For sure," I answered, "but like our conversation about Ben, we'll save it for another time."

"You still have the bug. We weren't fast, but we finished."

I studied Katharine. She was a beautiful woman, strong and confident. I wished her eyes held less pain. Perhaps she thought the same of me.

"Can you to tell me about Jim?" she asked.

"Jim." Warmth moved through me, from the inside out. "He's an amazing man, and an even better detective. I met him about three years ago, I guess. He helped me through some very difficult times after my husband's death, then he was shot in the line of duty. I moved him in with me and he's been there ever since. Almost a year now."

"How's he doing?"

"Unbelievably enough, he still suffers from amnesia." I stopped and gazed at her, kicking myself for being so stupid. "You're a psychologist. You get this stuff."

She raised her eyebrows. This time, she waited for a moment, letting me decide if and how I wished to continue.

"There's something about you," I said. "About

us—we seem to have connected. I'm going to hate going back home. I'll miss you. A lot."

"I feel the same way." She glanced at a picture on the wall, then her eyes turned to gaze out the window.

"Oh, look at the time. Tomorrow?"

"It's a date."

I ordered a coffee after Katharine left. Dredging up old memories—worse, a flood of old feelings—had worn me out. I ached for Jon, my dog Rex, and my old life.

I spent the next half-hour in a fruitless attempt to shift my brain back to the present. Every time I tried to get caught up in the day in front of me, a magnet pulled me back to the past.

I wandered back to the car, grabbed my laptop from the trunk and went to a picnic table on the museum grounds. I fired up the computer and Googled directions to Quebec City—279 miles with an estimated travel time of six hours and twenty minutes. The trip would require an overnight stay at the least. But first, I needed more information. Like whether or not Stitsill's kids lived in Quebec or somewhere else. I remembered Lucas Sweeney, the government agent who'd helped McGrath and I eliminate Jon's impostor. Surely, he'd have access to those statistics. He seems to know about everything like that. First, I had to remember the daughter's name. Sweeney and McGrath had both searched for her before, but so much time had passed. Maybe she'd ducked out of sight for a while, but had resumed her life now that both my husband and her father were dead.

I searched my phone contacts for Sweeney's number. While I hadn't spoken with him in over a year, I assured myself he would not only take, but welcome my call. You couldn't share a harrowing experience like we'd shared in Japan and not be happy to reconnect. Like soldiers who'd fought the same battle, we were bound by survival.

No time like the present. I dialed his number, wondering as the call connected if he still worked in Japan. If he did, I was phoning him late at night. At least not the middle of the night.

His number rang six times before going to voicemail. I left a simple message. "Hi, Lucas. Samantha Stitsill here. Sorry I haven't been in touch sooner. I'm somewhat embarrassed—I'm calling you because I need a favor. If you could call me when you have the chance, I'd be most appreciative."

I disconnected and sat for a moment, forcing air in and out of my lungs. I'd been here before. If only I could be content with the status quo. But searching was what I did best. Wanting more.

I tipped back my head and drank in the sunshine. The cloudless sky could mean I was on the right path. Where I needed to be. In spite of my racing heartbeat, a sudden peace engulfed me. A realization dawned in that moment. I had become like my intuitive friend Di. I was having feelings about things. Or maybe, maybe I was simply learning to trust my gut.

God help me.

CHAPTER FOURTEEN

MCGRATH SURPRISED ME by kissing my sweaty neck.

"What are you so engrossed in?" he said. "Did you have a good run?"

I chose to focus on the second question, rather than the first.

"Great run. Where's Ben?"

McGrath chuckled. "Guess he trusts me on my own. Now that I'm the summer guest artist, he must not feel the need to usher me around any longer."

"If that's the case, I agree wholeheartedly. You're certainly no longer in need of a chaperone."

He kissed me again. "Let's do something to celebrate."

"What do you have in mind?" His dimples sent a shiver up my spine.

His look said it all.

"I'm going to need a shower first," I said.

He winked and grasped my hand. "I like showers," he answered.

"Oh, boy."

I packed up my gear and we scurried to the car. As soon as I'd settled in to the passenger seat, my phone rang. Sweeney.

"Who's that?" he asked.

I remembered how things had gone south with Jon. We'd stopped talking to each other. Stopped sharing the most important parts of ourselves, and eventually came to leave out the small details as well. I'd vowed never to make the same mistake with McGrath, yet I hesitated to bring him into the entire Stitsill situation. He was just regaining his memory, his self-reliance, his sense of self. I didn't want to cause a setback.

My stomach knotted. "Lucas Sweeney. I'll call him back later. It'll be a long conversation."

"That's weird. We haven't heard from him in a long time." He paused. "How long has it been?"

"The last time was right after we got home from Japan, so…a year or so?"

"Almost two years. That's a long time. I wonder what he wants." McGrath wound his way through the park.

"I don't know," I lied.

I spent the next twenty minutes figuring how and when I'd call Lucas back, along with kicking myself for lying to McGrath. I better sort out those missteps soon—before I screwed my life up again.

After our shower we spent the rest of the

afternoon climbing Gorham Mountain. The trek brought back memories I'd shelved long ago. Jon and I had visited Acadia National Park when the kids were small and climbed this very mountain, one of the shorter treks to the top, and manageable for little legs. I'd slipped on the way down and sailed through the air for a good twelve feet before landing flat on my face in the dirt. I put on a brave mask in front of my four small children, but I barely made the remaining descent, my guts in my throat.

I watched my steps closely today. If I was smart, I'd carry the same message into my immediate future.

After our second shower of the day, we meandered down the road, yes, we meandered, to a lobster pound, which sat right on the water. Quite simply, the view was majestic. The sun began to set over the water, casting an orange glow on both the sea and sky, which met in a splendid smooth line. Peaceful. And romantic. The angst of the day faded to the background and I turned every ounce of my attention to McGrath and his smiling eyes.

"Tell me more about carving. What does a guest artist do exactly?"

"I'll spend time carving with some of Ben's students. Show them my approach to the art, and guide them through a simple carving."

"What's easy to carve?"

"I'll start them out with a 4-inch piece of basswood. Soft wood is best for beginners."

"Can you show me?"

McGrath's bracketed smile set his dimples deep. "Be right back." He darted off to the woods. He arrived back at the table five minutes later with a small round of pine, perhaps three inches in diameter. He moved his lobster basket aside, cleared a small workspace and produced a knife from the pocket of his khaki's.

As he moved the knife over the bark, expertly removing the covering, it was as if I were listening to a musician create a song. The soft scraping of the blade over the wood seemed rhythmic somehow, like the bass in a lively melody. But what really struck me was his concentration. He entered another world as soon as he put the knife's edge to the wood. He screwed up his face, and I saw him as a little boy. Nick used to make a similar face when he built with Legos. I hoped I'd still be able to see Nick as a youngster when he was a man, and was struck again by the magic bond a mother has with her children, having known them longer than they've known themselves.

After stripping the bark, he gazed at me, as happy as I'd ever seen him. "Now," he said, "I imagine what I want to carve. With a student new to carving, I'd show them a sketch, and ask them to copy the image onto their wood."

My heart swelled with pride, and I reached over and ran my finger along the back of his hand. "Ben said you don't use a sketch or a model of any kind. I can copy, but coming up with something on my own is impossible."

McGrath grasped the ordering pencil from a nearby table and began to sketch on a clean napkin. He drew a Santa, which made me laugh—the rendering reminded me of Ben. Next, he handed me the wood and the pencil with one direction, "Draw."

"Me? I couldn't." Still, I lifted the pencil to the wood, and began to etch lines. After fifteen minutes or so, I admired my work. "Not bad." I showed McGrath, who sat like a proud papa, focused on my every stroke.

"Good work." He patted my shoulder.

"Now what?"

"You're going to make cuts in the wood. Start just below Santa's hat, here."

My eyes pleaded with him. I was scared shitless.

He frowned and waved a dismissing hand. "What are you worried about?"

"What if I screw up?" I whined.

"This is not a test. You're practicing. With practice and determination, you can do anything you set your mind to. I've heard you say that to the kids a million times."

"And to my students."

"Then listen to yourself, teacher. C'mon, let's get moving."

I began to make small, tentative cuts in the wood.

I figured, if need be, I could cut deeper later. Carving was like cutting hair—I couldn't put the wood back if I took too much off.

I studied McGrath.

"Slice," he ordered.

I sought his approval after each cut. He watched encouragingly. I hadn't been the recipient of this type of attention for a very long time. Years, in fact. His care was unnerving, but in a good way.

"You're doing great," he said. "Think of this. You're defining the lines along the bottom of the hat, then you want to make extended slices along the bridge of his nose, longer and deeper."

I giggled like a schoolgirl.

"Good. Next you'll cut a stop at the bottom of his nose, followed by a slice cut up to the stop, so you'll wind up removing the chip below the nose."

I saw the vision in my mind's eye, and the wood gave beneath the blade. The finished product might pass for a Santa. McGrath talked me through the process, right until I shaped Santa's hat and beard.

"Now look at that!" McGrath beamed as he had after teaching me how to shoot.

"Funny how everything I learn from you involves weapons."

McGrath grimaced. "What do you mean?"

I'd forgotten that his memory wasn't completely intact yet, and although I'd agreed many months ago not to fill him on his past, I took exception now, considering he had recovered some small pieces of his life.

"You taught me how to shoot a gun. A long time ago. We went to your range, The Firing Line, I think it was called." I chuckled at the memory. "I took my first shot and we had to pay an extra $15 for the hole I made in the ceiling."

McGrath sat back in his chair. Pensive. "I remember."

I couldn't decide if he was sad, or thinking, or actually remembering. As much as waiting killed me, I did. For what seemed like an eternity.

Finally, McGrath, who'd wrung his hands to an unnatural shade of white, spoke. "I was so attracted to you. More than that—I fell in love with you at first sight. I hated knowing you were married. How could you have entered my life after I'd been alone for so many years, the girl of my dreams, and been married?"

Heat rose up my cheeks. In the glow of the moonlight, I blushed. Love at first sight hadn't been an option for me. I only remembered feeling conflicted. I was a married woman with five kids—an ordinary woman with an ordinary job, and this hot guy had my blood flowing. I'd swum a few hundred miles worth of laps, trying to ward off those feelings. Two years later, I was considering marrying this man. Everything happens for a reason, I reminded myself. But then I remembered Jon, and my heart ached again. I never intended for him to die.

Dinner revisited my throat.

"You okay?" He asked.

I bit my lip. "Just reliving moments I'd rather not."

"Meeting me wasn't fun for you, was it?"

"The timing was off, is all. But those days are behind me now. I can't go back."

"Would you do anything differently if you could?"

"Seems silly to second guess myself. I do enough of that without prompting, thank you very much."

"I understand," he said. "Sorry."

"Don't be sorry. The important thing is, your memory is returning. And you knew I was the girl for you right from the start. You ain't so bad yourself, Detective."

"Glad you feel that way, ma'am." He smiled and leaned back in his chair, just the way he'd done when we'd stopped for a burger two years ago, after the fated session at the range. Conflicted or not, there was no longer good reason to deny how I felt about this man.

"I have the serious hots for you." I bent over the arm of my chair and bracketed his face with my hands. "I love you. Pure and simple." I planted a firm kiss on his lips.

"Let's get out of here."

***

Two hours later, curled up in the dark, I asked him, "Has Ben said anything about Katharine? Do you have a feel for what's going on between those two?"

"He changed the subject when I told him the two of you were running this morning. Ignored me completely. Weird."

"She said they haven't spoken in about five years. Something happened. Something big."

"Ben plays life very close to the vest. He doesn't wear a wedding ring, but that's not surprising considering he's a woodworker. A lot of artists remove their rings when they work."

"I used to take mine off all the time," I said, gazing at the stucco ceiling, "and I'm not an artist."

McGrath continued. "Interesting. When we're together, we chat about the weather, sports, guy stuff, but nothing of merit. Not unusual for guys, as you know, but there's a sensitivity about the guy which leads me to believe he'd be more forthcoming than he is. Mostly, he seems interested in me."

"Sort of like he's the detective and you're the perp," I mused.

"Yeah, sort of."

"Does he probe?"

"I wouldn't say so. Now that you mention his avoidance technique, he's pretty skilled. He'll ask me questions about my carving mostly. Like, 'where'd you learn to do that?' and 'how long ago did you start carving?' knowing all the while that I've lost my memory. But he sticks to carving, doesn't get personal. Except for telling me how great he thinks you are."

"Really? He talks about me?"

"Face facts, Sam. Most people do. You look like you're about thirty years old, you have the body of a model, and you're pretty and smart. A guy'd have to be blind not to notice."

"He said something about how I looked?"

"Classy guys don't say those things directly, but trust me, when a guy mentions how lucky I am, I know what he means."

"Oh," was all I could say for a moment. "Do you think you can get him to open up about Katharine?"

"Good question. I've interrogated lots of tight-lipped folks over the years, but this guy's tough. He'd make a fine POW—he'd never give up his secrets."

I snuggled into McGrath's shoulder. "Do you think he served in the military?"

"I'm not sure," McGrath said. "But you said his dad was a cop. His dad may have been military, or maybe he even served. I could certainly mention my service and see if I can get a lead in, open him up."

"Perfect. If I accomplish nothing else on this trip, I'm going to solve the Katharine and Ben mystery."

"God help us," McGrath joked before kissing me

on the forehead, rolling over, and falling asleep.

CHAPTER FIFTEEN

SUNLIGHT FILTERED THROUGH the shades and I listened to the hum of the air conditioner as I woke. Friday. Last day visiting the museum this week. I glanced at the clock. 6 A.M. Early. Too early. But I was awake and the deck with its view of foamy waves and blue sky was inviting. I snuck out of bed without waking McGrath, and slipped into a pair of heavy sweats. Rather than walk over to the coffee depot in the main hotel, I used the room coffee maker. The sludge tasted horrid, but was warm nonetheless.

I finished my first cup, relaxing and settling into a few peaceful moments where my mind just played over the scenery and the smell of the salt air before I realized now would be the perfect time to return Lucas Sweeney's call. My arms buzzed like an electric current ran through them.

I tiptoed inside and unplugged my phone, careful not to make a single sound. I even inched the heavy wooden door to the deck closed and made a mental note to speak softly. I dialed and held my breath.

The call rang an interminable five times before Sweeney picked up.

"Sam, how are you? I've been meaning to call for some time. How does time get away like this? Are you well?"

"Yes. Perfect," I replied. "Jim and I are spending some time in Maine. He's regaining his memory, which is the most amazing thing. I think there's an excellent chance he'll be back to his old self soon, maybe even well enough to resume working."

"I heard about the shooting. But good news on the recovery front. Congratulations!"

"Thanks. Hey, I need a favor." I closed my eyes and thought about how to present my request. Hell, what was my request? I glanced at the room door, checking for any signs of movement inside, then began telling Sweeney my story, starting with Sir Harry Oakes, finishing with trying to locate Stitsill's daughter in Canada. I half expected Lucas to tell me I was crazy and say he wouldn't help me, but he didn't.

"Give me her name again. I should be able to search without a problem. Hell, you may even be able to find her as easily as I can."

Why hadn't I thought of that? "Her name is…Judy." From out of thin air, I remembered. "I don't know if Jon ever told you about her during the entire hullabaloo, but she phoned our house and spoke to him at length, thinking he was her father. And after Rosie Stitsill introduced herself to me, believing I was married to her dead husband, I ordered the guy's death certificate. The informant's name was Judy Stitsill. But Stitsill wasn't dead."

"Slow down, Sam. I remember most of this. You told me at the noodle shop in Nagoya, remember?"

I chewed on my bottom lip between sips of coffee.

"How about this?" Sweeney continued. "Let me see if I can connect the dots here." He sounded like my Jon. A process guy.

"How long do you think this will take?"

Sweeney answered my question without showing any signs of frustration. "I'm not sure, but let's say a week. I know that seems like a long time for someone like you, but try to relax and enjoy your time in Maine. We'll figure this out. And even if we don't, what would knowing change?"

"Good question," I admitted. "But if so, think about the coincidence. I wound up in this hotel where a direct link between the Stitsill mystery and the Sir Harry Oakes murder existed?"

"I guess stranger things have happened, Sam. But you're right. The likelihood is pretty astronomical." A pause, then Sweeney asked, "How are the kids?"

"Growing like crazy. The girls are driving now."

"Doesn't seem possible. I remembered the photos Jon showed me. They were still kids two and a half years ago."

"Happens fast," I admitted. "Too fast."

"All right," Sweeney said. "I'll be in touch."

"Thanks," I said before ending the call.

I tipped back my head, letting the sun warm my face, and said a prayer. Wrapping up the Stitsill mystery, and maybe even the Sir Harry Oakes mystery, all at the same time, seemed like a possibility. If I smoked, I'd celebrate with a cigarette.

I glanced at my phone. Only 6:30 A.M. Still plenty of time before we had to head to Southwest Harbor. I snuck inside and pilfered my laptop. I had to drape a towel over my head and the computer screen so I could see the damn thing, but I was able to Google

Judy Stitsill. My stomach began to flip-flop and my fingers jittered above the keyboard as I waited for the screen to load.

I about fell out of my chair once the information filled the screen. A full profile popped up. Evidently Judy Stitsill, whom we'd lost track of a couple of years ago, lived in Quebec City. She'd once lived in the Midwest—at an the address about forty miles from my home—according to the myhistory.com listing I viewed, but I had never been aware of that. Why hadn't I researched her before? Shame on me. Guess I did need those Private Eye courses after all.

She'd married a guy from Canada. Her name had changed. Judy Culver now. As I read on, I was glad I hadn't ingested anything more than coffee. When I'd spoken with Rosie at parent-teacher conferences the first night, she told me her husband Jon had originally been from Canada and had four daughters who still resided there. Now, on my screen, along with the info about Judy, 44 years old, I read about the other three sisters, Sarah, 42, Marlowe, 41, and Rachel, 40. Despite the thickness of my sweats, I couldn't stem the chills. I'd found her. All on my own.

I continued reading, rubbing my arms in a feeble attempt to warm myself and calm my nerves, but my jitters wouldn't subside. They worsened, in fact, as my eyes scrolled down the screen. The names of the girls' parents were listed. Not only did Jon's impostor's name appear, but the name of the kids' mother appeared as well. It was Betty. And Jon's mom, my Jon, her name was Betty. No one is named Betty nowadays. Well, I guess some women are, but I mean, really, my husband's identity is stolen and the guy not only assumes my husband's name, but now I discover his kids and wife have assumed the surname Stitsill and his former wife has the same name as my late mother-in-law.

When I felt a tap on my shoulder, I not only screamed and jumped, but kicked over the table and spilled coffee all over myself. "Shit, you scared me half to death!"

"What are you doing out here?" McGrath had saved my laptop from diving off the deck, helped me right the table, grabbed the towel, and began dabbing at my lap.

"I've been working on my computer. I couldn't see the screen. Don't ever scare me like that again. Do you understand?"

I clutched the closed laptop to my chest. I couldn't risk being found out. Not when I had this much new information in my grasp.

He approached and wrapped his arms around me. "Sorry, honey."

I reminded myself to breathe, and took in a measured lungful of air. "Jeesh. You startled me. Guess I still have some PTSD myself."

"My fault," McGrath admitted. "I, more than anyone, should understand the element of surprise is a no-go for folks like you and me."

I laughed finally. A welcome release. "I've reached my quota for surprises. Enough for a lifetime," I admitted.

"It's getting late," he said. "Are you coming with me this morning? You have a run scheduled with Katharine, right?"

"Oh, crap. We need to move along."

I hurried inside, tucked the laptop in my backpack and raced to grab a quick shower. I dressed in my running gear and slung my pack over my shoulder. I might have time to finish more research later. Though I'd discovered enough in those few minutes on the deck to last me a good long while. My craving for excitement had gotten me into trouble more than once. What I should do is leave the damned laptop behind, or toss the device in the ocean so I could have a normal life like most people.

On the ride to Southwest Harbor, I prayed that my chills would subside once and for all with my morning run. Spending time with Katharine would change my focus. *Thank you, God, for introducing us.*

I clung to McGrath. Not literally, but in my mind. *What the hell is wrong with me?* Rather than trotting off down the street after I'd said goodbye to him at the museum door, I trudged, exhausted.

Katharine sat on the bench outside the coffee shop, right where I'd found her yesterday. She wore a big smile and jumped up when she saw me. "Hey, running buddy."

I attempted a smile, but it was weak.

"What's wrong?" she asked, reaching out to touch my arm. I struggled not to pull away. A fallback position from my youth. Curling up in a fetal position and hiding under the covers when life got tough.

"Nothing a good run won't cure," I managed. "Let's hit the trail."

Katharine was as smart as I thought—she took off at a good clip and I struggled to match her stride. It was the perfect prescription for getting my mind in a different game. We ran for a good fifteen minutes before either one of us spoke.

"Thanks." I huffed.

Katharine slowed her pace a bit. "You're

welcome," she said, turning toward the beach path we'd run along yesterday.

We continued our run silently, an unspoken bond between us.

Back at the coffee shop, we stepped inside to order coffee and water.

"Great run," I said. "The cardio worked its usual magic."

"For me, too," Katharine said, as we snagged our regular table at the back of the shop. The slatted wooden floor squeaked as I sat down, and I took in my surroundings, reminding myself to slow down. The view of the pines out back settled me, along with the gentle whooshing of the espresso machine.

"Swimming is my magic of choice, but running takes a close second."

"You swim?" Katharine asked.

"Not in a long time," I admitted. "When my husband was still alive, for probably ten years or so, I'd get up at 5 A.M. on the weekday mornings when he was in town, and swim with my colleagues before school."

"You have a pool?"

"At the middle school where I teach. One of the perks in the building. The school was built as a dream in the eighties by one of the superintendents, then the district didn't have enough money to open the place, so they rented it to the military for a few years before finally getting the funds together. The usual education faux pas. We need more MBA's running the educational system, I swear."

"I hear you."

Katharine seemed distracted. I guessed her inattentiveness had something to do with Ben, but I wasn't about to prompt her on the subject.

"What do you have planned for the rest of the day?" I asked.

"I garden," she said.

"I can't keep anything alive long enough to have a garden," I admitted.

"Come and see the house," she suggested. "You can meet my husband, Paul."

I glanced at Katharine's ring finger, noting the absence of a ring. Hm. "Oh, I couldn't. I'm all sweaty and Jim will be ready to head back to the hotel in…" I paused to glance at my watch, then began to laugh. "In two hours."

"See? There's plenty of time, and Paul is accustomed to my alluring aroma. He'll never suspect you!"

"How far away are you?"

"Walking distance." Katharine handed me my coffee as she stood. "C'mon. Let's go."

I followed her out the door and down the street, into a charming residential neighborhood. On the front lawn in front of one of the many darling little clapboard homes sat a sawhorse table lined with jarred honey, with cute little "locally grown" stickers, and fresh loaves of bread.

No question. Southwest Harbor was a picturesque, storybook town. I feared once I entered Katharine's home, my image of this perfect little place would be tarnished. Reality would set in, and I'd have to acknowledge that Southwest Harbor was more than a place people went to escape their everyday lives. Plus, I yearned for Katharine and Ben to be together—in my mind, seeing each other would erase the pain in both of their eyes—their happy-ever-after ending making my dreams of this place complete. Probably not about to happen, as I was steps away from meeting Katharine's husband.

Plus, what business did I have wanting all this without knowing what they wished for themselves? Good Lord, woman, get a grip.

"We're here," Katharine announced, stopping in front of a lovely little cedar shake L-shaped home with a sloping roof that invited fairy tales to float through my mind. The soft brown of the shingles was brought to life by the yellow door and window trim. The style matched Katharine's personality, bright and sunny. Maybe Katharine did have a good life sans Ben.

"It's so sweet," I said. "Thanks for inviting me. I feel like we're friends already."

Katharine looped her arm through mine. "Because we are."

She led me up the path, opened the screen door,

and ushered me inside. "Paul's probably out on the deck. I'll introduce you in a few minutes. Let's do the grand tour first."

I strode inside, enraptured by the antiques, as if I'd stepped into the past.

"The place was built in 1932," Katharine said. "I've tried to keep the decor fairly authentic, although I will admit, some of the furniture—especially the sofa—is much newer than the style suggests."

"Elegant, yet comfortable."

I was in awe. What a talented woman I'd garnered as a friend. Planked oak floors with antique rugs, and wooden window casings flanked by cabbage rose curtains gave the living room a homey, cheery feel, and the built-in shelves on either side of the fireplace were filled with colorful pieces of glass.

"Sea glass," I said. "May I?"

"Of course," she said.

I stepped toward the shelves. Vases, bowls, antique jars, all full to the brim with sea glass. "How long have you been collecting this?"

"My entire life," she said. "As a girl, I'd make up stories with each new piece I found. Where the piece came from, who had last touched it, why I was given the gift of holding it my hands."

"Do you have favorite pieces?"

"How'd you guess?"

"I would, if I were you."

"My favorites are the cobalt blues, emerald

greens, and aquamarine. I love the bottlenecks, too. Here, I have an entire bowl filled with them. They're spectacular, aren't they?"

"Yes."

"Orange, blood red, and yellow are the rarest varieties. I have a jar right there." Katharine pointed to a tall urn filled to the brim with colorful shards.

"I'm stunned." I knelt before her collection.

"I'm fifty years old. I've been collecting since I turned eight. Every little treasure adds up." Her pride was contagious. "Plus, the search is therapeutic. After I lost the baby, I spent hours on the beach. Hunting for glass takes time and forces me to slow down. You can't run when you're sifting through sand," she admitted with a faraway gaze.

My mind cranked a four-minute mile. How long ago had she lost the baby? How long had she and Paul been married?

"Would you like a cup of tea?" she asked.

"Please," I said, as I pored over the pieces.

"I'll ask Paul if he'd like to join us, and then we can sit on the deck and enjoy the garden." Katharine trotted off to the kitchen, and I took a moment to peruse the rest of the room. A painting of a simple seascape hung on the wall, but there were no photographs. I pictured the photos that filled my walls and tabletops. The displays were all of my kids. And my folks and Jon. Family.

Maybe all childless couples were like that. No

photos. No memories. Or maybe Katharine didn't like photographs.

"Tea's ready," Katharine called from the kitchen. "Ready to go out on the deck?"

"Coming," I called, setting a jar of sea glass back on the shelf. The same sunny vibe lived in the kitchen. I gazed out the corner window at her yard. The beds spilled over with peonies, roses, hosta, and annuals, and spoke Katharine through and through. "This is beautiful," was all I could say.

"Grab your tea," Katharine said, nodding at an oversized mug on the counter. Then, she propped open the screen door with her hip and gestured for me to head out first. I spotted Paul sitting near the railing to my left. He turned his wheelchair when he heard us approaching, and steered over toward me, extending his hand as he did.

I smiled at him, trying to hide my surprise. Why hadn't she told me about him? How had he injured himself?

"Hi," he said, "You must be Sam. Kat's told me so much about you."

"Nice to meet you, Paul," I said, shaking his hand. He was a good-looking bald gentleman, trim and muscular, as if he spent a fair amount of time keeping his upper body toned. His large brown eyes were the focal point of his narrow face; flecked with gold, they were deep set and intelligent, and they lit up when he smiled. He expertly operated the power chair, scooting up to the table at a spot clearly designated for him by the absence of a chair.

"Tell me about yourself," he said.

I hate talking about myself. I opted for my usual recitation. "I'm a special education teacher. Got five kids at home, four teenagers. They keep me busy. What about yourself?"

"I'm an author," Paul said.

"Really," I said, surprised for a reason I couldn't name.

Katharine filled in the blanks. "Paul writes parenting books. We're both psychologists, but he's actually continued a small practice even after his writing career took off."

"I should know you," I joked. "I have five kids!"

"I write books for parents of special needs children, namely autistic kids."

"Wow," I said. "The three of us have so much in common. Fate must have brought us together." We discussed the pros and cons of aging for thirty minutes before I remembered McGrath had probably finished carving by now, and was most likely combing the streets searching for his missing woman.

"Look at the time," I said. "I've gotta run." I excused myself, making a plan to run with Katharine again on Monday, and agreeing with Paul that the four of us should have dinner soon.

"We're staying at The Willows. We love the Jack Russell, right across the street."

"There's a great lobster pound, Thurston's, just about ten minutes from here. Right on the water. Great value, beautiful sunsets," Paul offered, reaching out to touch Katharine's arm.

If I wasn't imagining things, she pulled away when he touched her. Just enough for me to notice.

"I'll see myself out," I said. "We'll have to wander through the house and garden next time I come. I'm still dying for the grand tour."

Katharine nodded. "Can you find your way back to town?" she asked.

"I think so. Then again, if not, Jim's a detective. He'll find me."

I left through the front door, easing it closed behind me. On my short walk back to town, I thought of Paul and Katharine, questions popping like heated kernels in my brain.

CHAPTER SIXTEEN

B Y THE TIME I arrived back at the museum my brain was on overdrive. Maybe McGrath had found out something about Ben and his past. I spotted him at the picnic table out back.

"Hey there," he said, his dimples deepening.

I settled on his face and a sudden peace filled me. I remembered this feeling from our first meeting: a combination of electric sparks and the comfort of being with an old friend. I let those feelings wash over me now, and settle me down. Between the news about the impostor's daughter and her family and the morning spent with Katharine and her husband, I deserved a few relaxing moments lost in McGrath's company. I exhaled a long puff of air, rested my head on his shoulder, and inhaled his spicy scent.

"I love being with you. You calm me down. Bring out the peaceful side of me that I seldom allow to rise to the surface. Thank you."

"You've always done the same for me. When we sat on the deck of that burger joint along the river that first afternoon we spent together, I remember the contentment I felt. I never recall having felt that way before. You do good things for me, Sam."

"You're coming back to me," I said as tears welled, my skin softening beneath his touch. I shook my head in disbelief. "I worried you wouldn't, and we'd forge a life together, but miss huge clumps of our history."

"Would have been a damned shame," McGrath said. "I don't know about you, but remembering those first moments together brings the feelings back. The tingle in my veins, the quickening of my heartbeat, all of the magic. It fills me up."

"You're waxing poetic." I grasped his hand and squeezed. "We're finding our way back to us."

"Want to go ring shopping?"

"Maybe," I said, "but first I need a shower."

"You sure require lots of cleaning," McGrath said as he patted my rear. "I can help if you'd like." He rested his hands on my shoulders, backing me away from him and giving me the once over. "Yes," he said, "you're a god-awful mess. You're definitely going to need help."

I stood, poised to race for the car. "First one back gets their choice of sides."

"Sides?" McGrath looked puzzled.

"Back or front? Which would you like to lather first? You've gotta beat me to the car to win."

McGrath sped past me.

***

We wandered into town hours later, settling for a lobster shack on the water where we could belly up to the bar, sit knee to knee and focus on our own little world for a while. "If we could travel anywhere in the world, just the two of us, where would you like to go?"

I clinked my glass to his, then said. "Italy. Wine and pasta."

"Honeymoon?"

"Sounds perfect."

"What type of ring should we be looking for? Do you want a huge rock? Not that I can afford one with my current finances, but we can dream, right?"

I wondered then how much time would pass until he could return to work, and whether or not he'd want to return to his own place for a while, now that he'd regained a good deal of his memory. He was still occupying Lizzie's room at my place, Lizzie sharing the master bedroom with me. I didn't feel right exposing the kids to our sexual relationship before we were legally hitched.

"A simple band will suffice," I said. "The love matters, not the ring."

"God, I love you," McGrath said, the worry lines easing from his brow.

"I'm thinking a year from this fall," I said.

He stuck out his bottom lip. "Why wait?"

"You'll need time to settle back into your job. The kids will need time to become adjusted to the idea."

"May I remind you we already function as a family? They're used to me, Sam. They love me, I think."

"They definitely do. But, hey, doesn't it feel good to put a plan in place? Time flies, remember?" I thought about my goal to take classes and get my Private Investigator certification. "I've also made some plans I need to share with you."

I told him about my scheduled community college classes for the fall and my request for time off to complete my studies.

"Are you sure that's what you want? You're a born teacher, Sam. I can't imagine you doing anything else."

"I'll admit," I said, "I've wavered some since I wrote the email to HR. But I know how I loved helping you with your cases, and you've confessed a number of times that I have a knack for solving puzzles."

He shivered, and the temperature didn't warrant his chill.

"What's the matter?" I asked.

"I hate the thought of you putting yourself in danger. Think. Your kids already lost one parent, and you've experienced a couple of close calls over the past two years. Seems like you've managed to get yourself in the thick of things without a PI license. Are you really up for this? Plus, most cases are boring surveillance. Tedious hours stalking the unfaithful, gathering information. Not at all the intrigue and excitement you imagine."

That got my back up. "I thought you'd be supportive."

McGrath placed his hand over mine. "I'll support whatever decision you make. You know I will. I just want you to know what you're getting yourself into. Plus, I still have to sort out my own life."

"Will you return to the force?"

He sank back in his chair and scrubbed a hand over his face. "Guess I have a lot to think about, too, don't I?"

"We don't have to decide today." I paused to study him. His brow had creased, worry settling back in. "Tell me about your morning. Did you gather any dirt on Ben?"

"I tried, but the guy's a diversion expert. I've interrogated hundreds of people, and he's as tough as they come."

I leaned into him and whispered, "Which makes me think he's got something to hide. Why wouldn't he just give you the facts?"

"Look who's talking." McGrath twirled a lock of my hair around his finger. "You don't let anyone in."

"Now, that's not exactly true."

"What have you shared with your new friend, Katharine? I'll bet not much."

"No." I shook my head and took a sip of beer. "I've told her I have five kids, I lost my husband two years ago, and I teach special education."

"Very revealing." McGrath's eyes twinkled.

"She's fascinating."

"See? There you go again, changing the subject. You're as bad as Ben."

"Not true. Not true at all."

"Then tell me something you haven't told me before—something about you I don't already know**.**"

I spun on my barstool, thinking. "I used to sing with a rock and roll band."

"What? You've been holding out on me. Now you're even more attractive."

"Really," I mused. "Why?"

"Rock and roll singers are sexy. What band?"

"My brother Mark played in a band in college, Twisted Vines. I sang with them for a few months when their lead singer couldn't make their gigs."

"What did you wear?"

"Singer clothes, of course."

"Singer clothes?" McGrath spun a three-sixty on his stool and whistled. "Do you still have them? Will you model them for me?"

I shuddered. "Garb from twenty years ago? I think not."

"C'mon."

"All right," I said. "Enough about me. Your turn. Tell me something about you now."

"I lost my memory, remember?"

"Cheater," I exclaimed.

McGrath took that as an excuse to use the facilities. I toyed with the idea of sharing my discovery about the possibility of a Stitsill/Marigny connection, and the startling news about Stitsill's children, but the idea seemed risky. It made more sense for me to plan a side trip to Quebec while McGrath was busy teaching at the museum. I could explain my excursion as a visit to place I'd always wanted to go. But what if he remembered Stitsill's Canada connection? What if he balked at me traveling without him? What if I told him Katharine and I were taking a road trip? Could I lie to him?

Maybe.

Two opposing voices. One telling me life unfolds just as it's meant to. In the end, changing our actions or decisions wouldn't have made a difference. Que sera sera. And the other telling me the reason for mistakes is to learn from them and not repeat them. Didn't seem likely I'd ever learn that particular lesson.

I pored over my options. I could drive to Quebec when McGrath was busy at the museum—if I left at the crack of dawn, I could make the trek in two days. McGrath would only have to spend one night alone. Maybe he and Ben could arrange to meet for a beer, or better yet, dinner. My mind spun like a $3 top.

What would be my reason for taking off without him? I didn't have to tell him where I was headed, did I?

Of course, I did.

I drummed my fingers on the bar. *Think, Sam. Think.*

I need time alone? So not true. I couldn't create a plausible explanation. We were just getting "us" back.

McGrath's lips on my neck about caused me to jump off my stool.

"You're lost in thought," he said. "What now?"

"Oh, nothing," I said. "Just trying to figure out Ben and Katharine."

"What's running through your head?"

"Katharine's husband is a paraplegic. Maybe she fell into Ben's arms because Paul's equipment is, well, for lack of a better word, busted. He's a nice guy and all, but living without sex…"

"Is impossible for a hot woman such as yourself to imagine."

"Precisely," I said. "She and Ben could have had an affair. Then, let's say Paul found out and put the kibosh on their trysts. Or maybe she'd hired Ben to donate sperm so she could have a kid, and then she lost the baby, and that's why they seem so tied to each other."

McGrath tossed his head back and rolled his eyes before he ordered two more beers. "There's chemistry or some deep personal connection, right, Detective

Stitsill?"

"You haven't met Katharine yet, but I assure you, something profound happened between those two. And, so, why aren't they together? Ben's not married, right?"

McGrath shrugged and toyed with the ring finger on my left hand. "We've talked about this. Not everyone who's married wears a ring."

"Still, you've been carving with him all week, just the two of you, and he's yet to share anything personal with you."

"Guys, Sam. We can shoot the shit for years. We aren't like women. We don't feel the need to share our innermost secrets right off the bat, or ever, for that matter. Even as guarded as you are, when you have a close friend, like Di, for instance, you share on a much deeper level than I ever would with a friend. The closest, deepest relationship a guy ever has is with a woman."

I frowned. "Because of sex."

"It's not a bad thing." McGrath brushed my breast with his fingertips.

McGrath had never shared a close relationship with a friend for as long as I'd known him. He knew guys on the local police forces, but he never spent hours on end with them, just met for the occasional beer, or talked sports while working out at the gym. Since his accident, he'd only been with the kids and I. He and Ed had formed a friendship of sorts, but didn't spend any real time together other than to fix the lawnmower or mend a screen door.

Jon hadn't ever spent a great deal of time with friends either. But growing up, my brothers had tons of friends. They buzzed around our house like flies in August. Neither Jon nor McGrath had siblings. Lone cowboys.

I'd never put those details together before, and it bothered me to think about Jon and McGrath in the same breath. I look a long draw on my beer.

"I need a cigarette," I said to no one in particular.

"What's wrong?" McGrath asked. "I thought I was distracting you."

I smiled weakly. "Sorry. Just thinking about gender differences."

"Like I said…"

"Okay, you win. Let's go."

CHAPTER SEVENTEEN

KYLE FOUND DETECTIVE James McGrath's residence on the Huron River, a quaint little well-kept bungalow. The good detective didn't seem to be home, and the way his house was situated, he had privacy on the riverfront, but not from the street. Nowhere to park and keep tabs on the guy's arrival home. With brain damage, he might be at rehab. Maybe he had a live-in caretaker.

Samantha Stitsill couldn't possibly manage his care while raising five youngsters.

Kyle drove to the end of the street and pulled a U-ey, then headed back past McGrath's place. He had spotted a canoe livery not far from the house, and pulled out one of his fake IDs so he could rent a boat for an hour or two and conduct surveillance from the water. Better yet, he'd pay for a full afternoon so he didn't have to rush. If luck served him well, he'd belly up to the riverbank and feign hunting for some kind of herbaceous wonder.

He strode into the livery restroom and changed

into some shorts and running shoes, careful to apply sunscreen to his exposed skin. Then, he pulled a ball cap over his head and adjusted his sunglasses to cover his eyes before tucking his clothing in the trunk of his car and heading inside to rent a boat.

Kyle paddled to McGrath's home within fifteen minutes of renting the canoe. McGrath's residence had a bit of a path worn along the shoreline, just enough to pull the boat out of the water and beach the boat. Two minutes later, Kyle climbed the bank and was standing behind a pine tree at the edge of the property. He pulled up his binoculars and cased the house.

No one appeared home, so he strode the hill to the house as if he belonged there, popped the lock on the back door, and entered the place.

Far neater than he imagined, but then again, a detective had to be somewhat organized. Nothing appeared out of place though. Not a coffee mug in the sink, a toothbrush on the bathroom counter, or a pair of pants slung over the bedroom chair. And on the dining room table, he discovered a stack of mail. He checked the dates of the postmarks. Over a week old. Someone had collected mail for the dude, but he hadn't been home in at least seven days.

Kyle took the news as a sign, and spent the next few hours ransacking the place. He left right before dusk, his loot in a plastic Ziploc bag, making sure he hadn't left any sign of his presence in his wake.

A smug look graced his face as he pulled the door closed behind him.

CHAPTER EIGHTEEN

COME MONDAY, BOUND and determined to figure out Ben and Katharine's story, I hurried to meet her for our run. In any case, solving their mystery would keep me in Maine and allow me time to plan my goals and the itinerary for my Quebec trip. I met Katharine outside the coffee shop at nine o'clock sharp. The weather was cloudy, drizzly, and cold. Early morning blood-freezing cold. I couldn't warm up.

We fell into a rhythmic stride, easing into our running pace. Both of us were quiet, and I tossed our silence off to the weather and the time of day. Nobody loves Monday. Finally, after ten minutes, Katharine spoke up.

"So, what did you think of Paul?"

"He seems great," I said, unsure what she was really asking.

"Were you surprised? I sometimes tell people about his accident ahead of time, but that gets old. I'd like to live my life without his chair being a topic of conversation all the time."

"I'm sure people are concerned."

Katharine shot me a disgruntled look. "Or just friggin' curious."

"About what?" I knew exactly what she meant, but decided to keep my own counsel, and let her vent.

We jogged toward the beach path, where the sand was wet and slippery. The drizzle continued and the wind picked up.

"Sex. Everyone wonders how we stay married when he's paralyzed from the waist down."

"Is this a new injury?"

Katharine slowed her running to a walk. She began to cry. After a long moment, she wiped her tear-stained face.

I waited.

"It's not a new injury. Rather an old one—getting older by the minute. We can have sex, but Paul's depressed and his libido's lost."

"That sucks," I said, pulling up my hood and taking her hand.

"I'm going crazy. I can't live like this."

I began to chuckle, and led her back towards town.

"What's so funny?" she asked.

"Nothing," I said. "I was just thinking how about how much trouble sex is. Whether you're having it, not having it, thinking about having it, it's not just about you— it's about your partner, too. I know God's supposed to be perfect, but he really messed up with sex."

"How are things with you and Jim?"

"Great, but for a host of reasons. Some perfectly reasonable, and some totally ridiculous. First of all, he's an exquisite lover. He has good pheromones. And I feel emotionally close to him and still seriously attracted to him, even since he lost his memory. Then there's the fact I have five kids who tag along most days.

"Don't get me wrong, I adore my children, but with the demands of motherhood, time for sex is at a premium, so we have to get the goods while we can."

Katharine arched her brows. "Guess the circumstances make a difference."

"Plus, we're not married. Sex is always better before you're married." Another good reason to put off the vows.

A far-away look crossed her face. "Paul and I have had some pretty hot sex."

Ah-ha. My big chance. "How long have you been together?"

"Married for ten years. Together for an eternity." She stated the facts with a fair amount of disdain. I didn't respond, just gave her time to formulate her thoughts, and decide what she wanted to share.

After a good sixty seconds, she continued. "We used to work together. School psychologists in the same district. We had an affair. He was married, I was not. And yes, you're right. The sex was much hotter when we were involved outside of marriage. Word of our affair hit the gossip mill. Neither one of us were skilled liars, so Paul left the schools and went on to earn his clinical license. By leaving the schools, he thought he'd minimize the injuries to my professional reputation, and perhaps be able to repair the damage to his own life. In a small town, though, there's little chance folks will forgive, much less forget."

"Sounds nasty," I said, passing her a sympathetic gaze.

"We stopped seeing each other once word spread about our affair. No contact whatsoever for almost two years."

I turned back toward the beach. Heading back to town and into the thick of her life didn't seem right.

"Was it agony being apart?"

"Not exactly." She bit her lip, and shook her head in disgust. "I'm not a very nice person."

"I like you."

"I was in a bad place. Horrid."

"Makes perfect sense."

"I'd tried to force Paul into making a decision. I couldn't bear for him to spend all the holidays with his wife, give her most of his time, and settle for the leftovers—too many broken plans, nights sitting waiting for the phone to ring. I gave him an ultimatum. Her or me."

"I'm not sure forcing him into a decision makes you an evil person."

"In the long run, I've ended up feeling like he had no choice but to divorce his wife and come back to me."

I paused at a park bench and sat, patting the spot next to me. Katharine settled in and fixed her gaze on the rolling sea. She murmured, "I involved myself with someone else, to make him jealous."

"Life happens."

"Thing is," she admitted, "I fell in love with the guy. Head over heels, soul mates forever kind of love."

She sounded miserable. I toed the sand with my shoe, scooping grains out and creating a small pile. "Did he feel the same way?"

"I think so. He said he did. But how can I ever know for sure?"

"I guess you can't." I waited for a full minute before I asked, "What happened?"

She continued to stare at the waves, her hair now matted to her head by the soft but steady rain, hands folded together so tightly her knuckles were parchment white.

"He was married, too. And he had an infant daughter. Then, I got pregnant. Of course, once I started showing, everyone thought I was expecting Paul's child. The buzz trailed me every time I left the teacher's lounge. The hum, deafening." She gazed skyward and her lips tightened into a thin line. "At that point, Paul and I hadn't spoken in months. With so many secrets, I was ready to explode."

I studied her, heavy with the weight of her confession and her agony.

"He had a wife and new baby. You could stay I stepped from the shallows into the deep blue sea."

At least.

"I delivered a full-term stillborn baby girl. All by myself. Without the baby's father. Without the love of my life. I no longer had the strength to fight. By then, Paul was divorced and swept in to clean up the mess I'd made of myself."

"I'm so sorry, Katharine."

Katharine tossed her head back as if to say, "What's done is done," and stood. "Let's head back to town. I'm freezing. You?"

The chilly rain had me craving a cup of hot tea. The conversation suggested I might need to throw in a shot of whiskey. I glanced at my watch. Probably no bars open yet.

"Cup of tea? Coffee?" I suggested.

"And then some." Katharine began to jog, and I joined her.

"I'm really sorry," I said.

"About what?" she asked.

"That you lost your daughter and the man you loved."

"Well," she replied. "We both know a fair

amount about loss, don't we?"

"We do."

We arrived at the coffee shop ten minutes later. The owner, a bearded, long-haired forty-something guy, took one look at us and grabbed two hand towels from behind the counter. We thanked him and began to dry off. He walked to the rear of the shop and plugged in a space heater near our usual table.

"Coffee? Tea?" he asked. "I'll serve you ladies today."

"Thanks, Scott." Katharine offered him a grateful half-grin.

Katharine ran the towel over her face, wrung out her dripping ponytail, then wadded the soaking towel between her hands, and set the cloth on the table. She glanced in the direction of the shopkeeper and offered an explanation. "Paul's accident brought new friends."

"How long ago?"

"Three years. He was hit by a car while jogging around one of the curves in the park. He'd done a stellar job keeping up his spirits, and managed to be upbeat for a long while. But then he hit bottom. Honestly, his writing has been a godsend. If he didn't have his books, I'm not sure he'd still be alive. His practice has helped too. He's felt an obligation to his clients to demonstrate his ability to rise above adversity."

"That's a ton of pressure." I couldn't imagine.

"I vacillate between being furious at him and

feeling desperately sorry for him."

I hesitated, but something told me to forge ahead. "You're rushing things. The two of you obviously care for each other. I can tell by the way you act. There's a softness that comes over him when he looks at you. And you return it. I understand you two had a less than ideal beginning and life has certainly been unfair to you, but maybe you can still make something of your marriage."

Katharine twisted her coffee stirrer into a bow and frowned.

"I'm saying this because I lost my husband. I wish I'd had a second chance. But you have to decide for yourself."

The front door squeaked open. I glanced over, distracted by the sound of the bell, and startled when I saw Ben enter the shop. A sudden unease swept over me. Katharine was vulnerable right now, and I had this overwhelming urge to jump in front of her like a human shield and protect her. Call it instinct. Call it intuition. Call it whatever.

She faced away from him and didn't wheel around as I had done. I quickly fixed my gaze on the table, hoping she'd miss the look of shock now covering my face. What was he doing here?

Out of the corner of one eye, I watched as he stepped up to the counter and ordered. I tried mightily to focus on my conversation with Katharine, but couldn't seem to get my bearings. Finally, she laid her hand atop mine. "What's the matter? You look as if you've seen a ghost."

"Just thinking about my late husband, Jon," I lied.

"Tell me about him," she said. "I've wallowed in my sorrows long enough."

I didn't feel like talking about Jon, but I'd backed myself into a corner. "It's complicated." Out of the corner of my eye, I watched Ben, bag of coffee in hand, leave the shop, and breathed a secret sigh of relief.

"What isn't?" She blew out a puff of air. "C'mon. Fair's fair. Your turn."

I hemmed and hawed. What would I feel comfortable sharing? Did I need to talk about Jon? Who did I talk about him with? Di, every now and then, but truth be told, I mostly held all those thoughts in my mind, vaulted with a combination only I possessed. When I had time alone with McGrath, I wanted to focus on the present and the future, not think about Jon.

"I hate talking about him."

Katharine settled back in her chair and crossed her legs.

"You're assuming a shrink posture."

"That's funny," she said. "Not your shrink. Just your friend."

The way she said the words reminded me of Jon. He would have said the same thing in this situation.

"Weird how life leads us down a certain path. One we have no notion of. No GPS system to let us know when a detour, slow-down, or road closure will occur." I sank back in my chair. After clenching my jaw, I continued. "Jon and I had created this life. We each had two young kids when we met, then after we were married a few years we decided to have a child of our own. Lizzie. She's ten now.

"Jon climbed the corporate ladder like a skilled acrobat, several rungs at a time." I blinked, remembering. "Effortlessly, in fact. We were financially secure, and I fooled myself into believing we had the perfect life."

I locked eyes with Katharine. She sat in silence, waiting for me to continue.

"He traveled all the time. I was lonely. The responsibility weighed me down, but I could never allow myself to admit I was cracking under the pressure. I worried if I confessed my shortcomings, my world would crumble. I had five little kids to care for, a full-time job, and a household to manage. And when Jon was home, I didn't want to ruin his life by complaining." I stared at my hands. "It's my own damned fault."

"What?"

"Shit," I said, "I don't know. I feel guilty all the time. It's a well-honed skill."

"Guilt is a woman's lot in life."

We shared a commiserating glance.

"If I let myself think about him, I miss him. I miss having a normal life. Not that ours was really a normal life, but it was normal for me, you know?"

"I get it."

"I'm sure you long for the days when Paul was healthy. Sort of the same thing."

"Definitely the same thing."

CHAPTER NINETEEN

I SPENT ANOTHER thirty minutes with Katharine before heading back to the museum. I needed some alone time, but the rain had picked up again and sitting outside wasn't an option. Pulling my hood tighter, I dashed down the street, snagged my backpack from the car and entered the museum display room. I found an out of the way bench to occupy, and fired up my laptop.

I'd bookmarked all the information about Jon's impostor's family as I discovered the details. I pulled the file up now, then Googled the address of the impostor's daughter, Judy Stitsill Culver. I logged the destination onto a spreadsheet, hoping to keep all the details organized in one place. It struck me as odd that Stitsill's kids shared his name. This man had stolen my husband's identity and one of the domino effects of the theft was the adoption of our surname to his offspring. Another piece of the puzzle I'd committed myself to solving.

I envisioned a three-day trip, but after

considering all the unknowns, a longer stay might be necessary. I considered asking Katharine to join me, but I couldn't imagine she'd believe my hypotheses, and I hated to ruin our friendship with a story that would perhaps frighten her—she'd consider me some crazy loon with whom she'd mistakenly entangled herself. Something told me that wouldn't be the case, but given my commitment to act less impulsive, I'd table the idea for a day or two before making a final decision.

I checked my email, perused a favorite online shopping site, then shut down my computer and headed to the workshop. The murmur of the men's voices provided me with reassurance, and as I'd grown accustomed to doing, stood silent in the doorway for a few moments, taking stock of the two men.

Ben leaned towards McGrath, his glasses poised on the tip of his nose, pointing out a line on the new carving. The room smelled of pine shavings, and the earth tones of the walls and the wood made the space welcoming. Soft flute music played in the background. James Galway.

"Danny Boy," I said, shivers traveling up my arms. My musician father had played the song for me when I was a young girl. The flute's eerie tone took me back. So far back a lump formed in my throat and tears rimmed my eyes.

The moment turned me upside down and inside

out at the same time. I missed my dad and longed for him like I hadn't in years. Since his death, I hadn't allowed myself to play the flute. Playing without him felt like a disservice to his memory, though I'd often played in solitude as a young girl. A stab of longing coursed through me.

"Yes," Ben said. "Do you like the song?"

"One of my favorites." I froze to the floor.

Ben glanced up and caught the stricken look on my face. "You could use a cup of tea," Ben said. "Come. Sit." He pulled out a stool, then walked over to the sink and filled a mug with water.

McGrath gazed up at last, having completed his final knife cut, and set down his work.

I swallowed hard, overcome by the depth of feeling the song had provoked. As Galway played the final note—a pure, valiant strain—some unearthly force zapped me. I sat down hard on the stool, steadied my chin in my palms and fought for breath.

"You okay?" McGrath asked.

"I need a moment. Seems you're not the only one recovering your memory."

I stayed quiet a few moments, trying to regain my bearings by focusing on a single wood scrap on the bench.

Ben set my tea on the table in front of me and laid a gentle hand on my shoulder. This guy had skills. If I didn't know better, I'd have claimed he was the one who held a psychology degree, not Paul. He reminded me of Mr. Miyagi from The Karate Kid. Wise. Strong. Tender. Intelligent.

"I'll be fine," I said, casting my eyes up with a weak smile. I cupped the warm mug in my hands, raised it to my lips, and sipped the life-giving medication.

"What happened?" McGrath asked.

"We can talk later," I said.

Ben broke the silence after an awkward moment. "Your friend here proved an impressive teacher this morning."

He jolted me out of my thoughts, and I remembered today was McGrath's first time with students. "How was it?"

"He's a born teacher," Ben said. "Adept at description and precise with his instructions. There's his sense of humor, too. We had a great morning." Pride lit up his face. "Tomorrow, he sees the seasoned carvers. They might prove more of a challenge."

I laughed with the two men before adding, "This man loves a challenge."

McGrath stood, brushed himself off, walked over and stood behind me, pulling me back to rest against his firm middle and resting his hands on my shoulders. "Got this girl to love me. If I can make that happen, I can work miracles like the man himself."

His eyes twinkled with satisfaction. He looked happy and strong.

When I finished my tea, we left Ben and drove

back to the hotel. The wipers slapped against the windshield and the rain came down in torrents, leaving us without the option of an afternoon hike. We decided to stop for a bite to eat and discuss plans for the remainder of the day. I parked the car on Main Street and we ducked inside McKay's Public House, another renovated Victorian home with rustic pine tables and chairs, twinkle lights strung across the bar, and a smiling young bartender. We each ordered the lobster mac and cheese and an ice-cold citrus ale. The chills I'd felt all morning finally abated, and I pumped McGrath about Ben.

"Is he letting you in at all?"

"Not really. But I did notice a photograph tucked under the glass on his desk." McGrath paused to scoop a healthy bite into his mouth.

"Seriously? You're going to drop a juicy tidbit into my lap and then take time to fill your face?"

McGrath grinned. All dimples. "I know how to get you going," he said, a long chew later.

"You're killing me here. Who was in the photo?"

"I only glanced. I didn't want to stare or make Ben uncomfortable. In the manual, guys are advised to respect each other's privacy. He'll tell me when he's ready."

"You have way more patience than me." I slid a forkful of cheesy macaroni into my mouth, then wiped my face with a napkin.

"And you're the special ed teacher. Imagine," he

teased.

"Would you please tell me?" I bit the inside of my cheek in anticipation.

"The picture was of a very pretty young woman and a baby."

"Girl or boy?" I asked.

"Pink blanket, so I'd say girl."

I thought about what Katharine had said. The man she'd fallen for had a wife and infant daughter. But that would have been eleven or so years ago. Wouldn't Ben have had a more recent photo of his wife and child on display? I asked McGrath's thoughts.

"Maybe," he mused. "Then again, if he placed the photo under the glass years ago, he may not have thought to update it. Guys are like that. The most likely scenario was that his wife gave him the photo and told him to put it on his desk at work. We follow directions well, but don't always display initiative."

I leaned back in my chair. I thought of Jon and how I used to frame photos of the kids and instruct him to place them on his desk at work. If I hadn't done so, his office would have been devoid of any signs of his family. "Point well taken."

We each ordered a second beer. "How are we going to figure this out? The guy doesn't share a lick with you about himself, he doesn't leave clues around. Do you even know where he lives?"

"I do, as a matter of fact," McGrath said. "He

lives down in Seawall. Small town on the water."

McGrath frustrated the hell out of me. He'd been a homicide detective. Didn't make sense that he'd lost the ability to ask a straight question. "If it were me, I'd just be direct. I'd ask him if he's married. Simple question. Simple answer." I paused and thought for a moment. "Did he say 'we' when you asked him where he lived?"

"Let me think." He shut his eyes. "Nope. Just said, 'Seawall.'One word answer." McGrath grimaced. "There's something about Ben that tells me not to ask about his family. I'd be intruding if I came right out and asked."

"What's the real risk, though? If he's put off, he'll get over it. He's a guy. Guys don't harbor grudges." I narrowed my eyes and peered at him, challenging him to question Ben.

He shook his head. Adamant. "He won't let me in—if I thought like you, I'd say he had a secret."

"Pretty profound, Detective. I'm impressed."

He chuckled. "Hey, I'm fully evolved. I've lived with you for almost a year now. You've rubbed off on me."

"I have an idea," I said, popping the last bite of lobster mac into my mouth. "Let's see if Paul and Katharine would like to meet us for dinner. The day's a wash out, and a double-date would give us something to look forward to. I have her number."

"Sure. Give her a call. I'd like to meet them."

When we arrived back at the hotel, I called Katharine and set up dinner at the Jack Russell across the street. After a quick shower and a long nap, I gussied myself up for an evening with new friends. Although the restaurant was right across the street, we decided to drive. The rain hadn't let up.

McGrath perused the bar as we walked inside, pointing out the framed photographs on the walls. "Dogs," he said.

I scowled at him quizzically. "You're a detective, right?"

"What's your point?" he asked.

"Those are Jack Russell Terriers," I said. "They're a breed."

"So the restaurant is named after a dog. I thought Jack Russell was a guy's name."

I rolled my eyes. "You're scaring me," I said. "I'll let it go this time, but if something like this happens again, I'm going to question my taste in men. I usually prefer someone of intelligence."

McGrath elbowed me, then kissed me on the cheek. "I guess I had that coming. I'll try not to disappoint you in the future."

"That would be best."

I scoured the bar area, but Katharine and Paul hadn't arrived yet. I asked the host for a low table, thinking of Paul and his wheelchair. We were led to a table in the far corner of the room, and I waved at Adam, the bartender, as we made our way to our seats.

"Blueberry blossom?" Adam called, a bit too loudly.

Knowing what I did about autism, I suspected Adam sat somewhere on the spectrum. His social skills were weak, but the kid was so darned friendly, you couldn't help but love him.

"Sounds delightful," I answered, "but you're going to have to turn on the fireplace if you serve me something on ice. Wicked cold out there."

Adam mumbled something under his breath about the weather, but I couldn't make out his words above the pounding rain.

McGrath and I snuggled into the corner chairs, leaving the outer spots for Katharine and Paul who had just entered the room. They joined us and we made introductions.

We spent the next two hours enjoying the food and company of our newfound friends. By the time we headed back to our hotel, we were glad we'd only had to drive across the street.

"I may have been over-served," I said.

"That bartender is in love with you."

"It's because I listen to him," I admitted. "Career hazard."

CHAPTER TWENTY

THE PHONE RANG early in the evening, so Judy didn't expect Kyle's voice. She chided herself for not having checked the caller ID. She knew better.

"Hi Kyle," she said. "You on your way?"

"No, not yet, but I'll keep you posted. You said the summer was free. Have your plans changed?"

"No, we'll be here. What's keeping you, if I may ask?"

"I spent a few days more doing more research, and discovered some interesting facts. Did you know Dad has two sons?"

Judy closed her eyes and hesitated. She opted for a flip answer. "He was a busy man."

"Way busy. His kids are young, like in middle or high school, and they live in Michigan."

"You're not thinking we need to meet these long lost relatives, are you?"

"I'm not sure. They're Mexican."

"You mean Hispanic."

"It's the same damned thing. Do you think Dad

has another wife around?"

"I have no idea. Look, Kyle, here's the deal. You are welcome to come and visit, but I have no desire to meet any of Dad's other sons. You're quite enough for me."

"Oh, because I'm trouble and you don't need any more?"

"No, you're taking my words out of context. I love you. I have my own family, too, and Dad's endless line of offspring is off-putting at this juncture in my life. Are you anxious to know them? Do you need another tie to Dad?"

"Maybe. Maybe not. If I found out he spent more time with them than he did with me, I'd probably be jealous."

"There you go. Leave well enough alone."

"But what if they have some of Dad's things?"

"Kyle, you have more sense than this. Every time something comes up around Dad, you turn into a five-year-old, hungry for any inch of him."

"Aren't you curious, though? Do you know if Dad remarried?"

"I don't."

"The kids were outside shooting hoops when I saw them. Their mom doesn't look Mexican. Do you think they're really Dad's kids? Maybe I should talk to them."

"Kyle, let's talk about this when you come to visit. Please, don't do anything silly. Think about how you would feel if a stranger approached you out of the blue and started talking about Dad. They may not even know he has other children, plus, you don't know if they even know Dad."

"I told you I researched. I Googled the Stitsill name and not only did I come up with Samantha Stitsill but Jon Stitsill too. Dad lived in Michigan. I found an address and a woman's name associated with him. Rosita Stitsill. You can see for yourself if you Google his name. You know how names pop up of people someone lives with."

Judy was astounded. Kyle's obsession with Dad hadn't been this bad in quite some time. And the reports of their father's death from Japan were legitimate. Dad was dead and gone. Resurrecting more of his ugly trail held no appeal. She'd finally moved past ever having been associated with him, and found a comfortable place to keep him, in the recesses of her mind, with a few treasured memories of the good times. But now, a flood of recollections came to mind. The sheer mention of Rosie's name brought back her years following Dad's path and pining for his love and attention, attending his wedding, making excuses for him with her sisters when he disappeared for months at a time. A stab of sadness gripped her. For her own peace of mind, she needed Kyle to leave this alone.

However, talking her immature, hyper, OCD, sociopath brother out of venturing down this road would be tough, if not impossible.

"You have a real family with me and the boys. Plus, I'm having a reunion party of sorts a week from Saturday. All the girls are coming with the kids. We'll all be together for once, and my mom would love to see you. She was asking about you the other day. Please come, Kyle. We miss you."

"I'm not sure. I want to stay here a little longer and see if I can find out more. I got a lead on where Dad worked. Maybe some of his friends can fill me in on his last few years. We didn't see him much then."

Judy pursed her lips. Kyle was right. They didn't see him much because he was supposed to be dead. She couldn't recall for certain, but Rosie had called her after dad's headless corpse was discovered in the family car. Judy knew better than to believe Dad had been killed, or committed suicide as the coroner ruled, but she went along with his ruse, because— because she'd been helpless to do much else. And Rosie, being a foreign national, had no idea how to negotiate the U.S. red tape.

Opening this web of lies and deceit was not on her to-do list this week.

"Judy, are you there?"

"Oh, yes. Sorry. Promise me something, will you?"

"What?" Kyle asked with a sarcastic edge.

"Don't bother those boys." She had to bite her tongue from saying their names. Joey and Emilio. She remembered them as infants and toddlers, but hadn't seen them in years. Hadn't heard from Rosie in years.

"I wouldn't bother them, I'd get to know them. You know, like a friend."

Judy swore her brother had multiple personalities, the way he could charm the pants off women one minute, engage in savvy business deals the next, and then morph into a child with a snap of the fingers.

"Kyle. Let's talk first. A week from Saturday. And please, come early. I could use help setting up the tent and the tables."

Judy crossed her fingers and prayed her sisters and mom were available for a spur of the moment family reunion. A gathering of the family was her only hope.

"I have a job to finish, then I'll head your way."

Judy let out a sigh of relief. "Great. I can't wait to see you."

Kyle ended the call and studied the clock in his room at the Marriot. Too early to return to the Stitsill house. But four hours from now, he'd be there. Seeing exactly where his dad's killer slept.

CHAPTER TWENTY-ONE

I AWOKE TO a dapple of radiant sunshine playing on my cheek and listened to the lonely sound of seagulls crying. I tiptoed out of bed, and, after brewing a cup of coffee, stepped onto the deck. While the coffee wasn't up to my standards, it was hot, and took the edge off the morning chill. The deck chairs were still damp from yesterday's rain, so I perched on the edge of the seat to look out to sea. A lobster boat puttered along, pausing every now and then to check its traps.

Katharine and Paul had seemed cozy last night, and Katharine much happier than she had yesterday morning. McGrath and Paul had talked guy stuff—food and sports. Paul recommended a long list of lobster pounds. Assuredly, we'd be visiting many of them over our remaining few weeks in Maine.

With the men busy bonding over large marine crustaceans, my damned impulses got the better of me—when I dropped the hint that I'd like to visit Quebec City, Katharine bit like a mosquito on plump flesh. I guessed she thought time away from Paul might provide them both with a much-needed break.

I remembered the initial years of Jon's travel. We'd always enjoyed and appreciated each other more having been apart a good deal of the time. His absences provided us with the opportunity to look forward to being together. I continued to rationalize my sneaky behavior, convincing myself I was doing her marriage a favor by tempting her to join me, until McGrath stepped out on the deck.

Sweetest man alive, he'd brought a towel and dried off my chair so I could sit back and relax. He'd also trekked across the parking lot and grabbed us some real coffee.

"I like Paul," he said, as I sipped. "And Katharine."

"It's nice having friends. We've been so busy with the kids, we hardly have time to socialize," I said.

His forehead creased as he sat back in his chair. After a long pause, he spoke. "I worry a little about Paul."

"Why?" The more time McGrath spent carving, the more his soul came to life. This introspective, compassionate side of him, which I hadn't often seen in the past, made him all the more attractive. I curbed my urge to tackle him right then and there and listened.

"He's struggling. Not that the edge he carries

doesn't make sense. I can't imagine losing the ability to walk. It's a manhood stripper, for sure."

"They can still have sex."

He raised his eyebrows and shot me a sideways smile. "Really? You ladies are discussing your sex lives?"

A blush rose to my cheeks. "She shared they're going through a bit of a dry spell, which leads me to believe this is a recent disruption. See? My investigative skills are improving."

"Still. As a fellow man, I'm just saying, we need to be able to walk. To saunter, in fact. To strut our stuff."

"It's that important to a guy? How sad for you, and for your entire gender." I offered him a disappointed frown.

"Seriously, Sam, I can't imagine." McGrath tented his fingers and pressed them together.

"So what you're saying is you'd take memory loss over paraplegia any day."

"Can't say that was the track I was on, but now that you mention the choice, most decidedly yes." He leaned over and planted a firm kiss on my cheek. "I can pursue you. All day long if I want. Paul…" He paused for a long moment, "he's gotta wrestle with his manhood each and every time he wants to make love with his wife."

"I understand. You're recovering from your amnesia, while Paul is looking at a lifetime in that chair. No chance for a miracle."

"All I know is, the loss of manhood would make me crazy. I'd rather be dead."

I set my coffee on the table between us and stood. "We'd better get ready for the day. I'm running with Katharine and you've got an early class, right?"

He nodded, patted me on the fanny, and made a happy little sound as if he'd just taken a delicious bite.

"By the way," I said, "while you and Paul were busy discussing world peace last night, Katharine and I discussed taking a road trip."

"A road trip?"

"Yes, you know, getting in the car and driving off to discover the great beyond. Girls on the run."

"Really." He became pensive.

"Just for a few days."

"That would be the first time we've been apart in almost a year."

I sashayed around and smiled at him, placing my hands on his morning whiskers and drawing him close. After a long, deep kiss, I said, "Will you miss me?"

"Definitely. But go. You haven't had time to do a thing for yourself in years, I suspect. Where are you headed?"

"Not sure," I lied. "Katharine and I are in the discussion phase. We have another four weeks here, so we're not in a rush or anything."

"Well, keep me posted," he said, glancing at his

watch. "Time for me to grab a shower."

While he was in the bathroom, I Googled "Marigny in Quebec." Low and behold, a healthy bit of information popped up. Even a link for Lac Marigny. My French was rusty, but I knew enough to know Lac meant a lake had been named for the Marigny's. Look out Quebec, here we come.

Alfred de Marigny had lived in Quebec for a few years before moving to South America. If my hunch was correct, he'd spent enough time there to father Jon Stitsill, the impostor. Don't ask me why I'd decided this was the case, but I trusted my instinct like I knew every crease and wrinkle on my face. Di would be proud of me. I was trusting my gut.

I pulled on my running duds and laced my shoes, my mind spinning. After my run, I'd drink a cup of coffee with Katharine, then head to the library to complete a little research. My plan was in motion. My pulse picked up speed.

***

As usual, Katharine waited on the bench outside the coffee house, wearing a bright smile.

"We had a great time last night," she said. "Although I must admit, I'm fighting a bit of a headache."

I tossed my head back and laughed, having noticed a twinge of hangover myself. "We had fun. I especially loved seeing Paul and Jim hit it off so well."

"Other than his colleagues, Paul doesn't have many friends," Katharine said. "Let's do dinner again soon."

We fell into an easy pace, both of us seeming much lighter than we had yesterday. A peaceful day after one of storms. The run felt effortless, my feet skipping across the pavement like stones across a calm sea. I accelerated into a full out run, and Katharine matched my pace.

"So, about the road trip?" she asked. "Are you serious?"

I nodded.

"I've been thinking—I'll drive so you don't have to worry about leaving Jim without a car. My schedule is wide open. When do you want to go?"

"I'm not sure." I wanted to have Judith Stitsill Culver's address before we left, and I hoped Lucas would get back to me and verify the information soon. I reckoned his sources would be more reliable than a search engine. I made a mental note to call him before I stepped into the library.

"Have you ever been to Quebec?" I asked. "I've always wanted to go. The last French I spoke was in my senior year of high school, but the challenge might be fun."

"Mais, oui, madame. Je parle un peu Francais."

"Guess I'm rustier than I thought. What did you

just say?"

"I'm not sure," Katharine admitted with laughing eyes. "I think I said, 'But yes, ma'am. I speak a little French. 'We'll have a grand adventure. Let's go."

Call me crazy, but I'm never happier than when I'm in the thick of a puzzle, and supreme contentment filled me now. I envisioned McGrath's dimples, and how I'd miss them—along with the warmth of his fingers as he stroked my bare skin. But only for a moment. I wouldn't be gone long, I reasoned, and I'd be so much smarter when I returned.

Katharine's laughter startled me.

"What?" I asked.

"You're running faster than ever. If I didn't know better, I'd guess you're the one who needs some time away, not me."

"Trust me, I was just thinking of how I'd miss Jim's dimples."

"Shit," she said. "The man is hot."

"Thanks. Paul's not bad either, you know."

Katharine thought for a full sixty seconds. "You're right," she said.

I pointed down the path to a wooden placard about a quarter mile away. "Race you to the beach sign."

We both took off. Full out. Laughing and kicking up sand with our heels as we battled to the finish. She finished a step behind me, but only one step.

"Not bad for old broads," she admitted.

"Not bad at all."

I said goodbye to Katharine at the coffee shop an hour after planning our next day's run. We tentatively planned to leave for Quebec the following Monday, which gave me six full days to prepare my to-do list. First thing, securing Judy's address. I dialed Sweeney as I walked down the street to retrieve my backpack and laptop.

He answered on the third ring, right before I remembered the time change.

"Did I wake you?" I asked.

"Not at all. I'm in the States for a bit."

"Oh," I said, startled. "Where?"

"I'd tell you, but then I'd have to kill you." His chuckle resonated with warmth.

"Really. Hush-hush, huh?"

"What can I do for you, Sam?"

"I wondered if you located Judy Culver. Stitsill's daughter…"

"Funny, I'd planned to call you a couple of days ago but got distracted." Lucas sounded more serious now. The change in his tone made me wonder what kept Sweeney so busy, and so preoccupied.

"And?" I popped open the trunk and rifled my backpack for a pen and paper.

"Hold on," he said. "I've loaded the address onto my phone. I'm going to put you on speaker so I can find the contact."

I leaned against the rear bumper of the rental and

waited. Sixty seconds later, I held confirmation of Judy's address in my hands.

"Thanks, Lucas," I said.

"You're very welcome, Sam." He cleared his throat and an awkward silence filled the line. "Do you mind if I ask what you have in mind? Anything I should know about?"

"Unanswered questions is all. Thought I might pay her a little visit," I said.

"You mentioned the possibility the last time we talked. I'd hoped you'd be past the idea by now."

"Is that the reason you never called me back? You wanted me to forget about her?" Men. They were all alike—fooling themselves into thinking they could control a woman.

"Not my business, but I'd suggest you let go of the notion. You have a good life now, don't you? With your detective and the kids? You deserve to put this behind you."

In all fairness, Lucas and I didn't know each other well, but as government agent, he knew human behavior. He'd figured me out before he checked the morning weather. His intentions were honorable. He wanted me to stay out of trouble.

"I promise to behave myself. I made a new friend in Maine and she and I are taking a little road trip is all. Just to satisfy my curiosity."

"You know what they say about curiosity," Lucas cautioned.

"Warn myself about that all the time." I paused and took a breath. "Thanks for the info, Lucas. I've gotta run, but take it easy."

"Sam?" he said.

"Yes." I waited, expecting a lecture.

"Be careful," he warned. "And give me a call if you need anything."

My heart warmed at his concern—I was sure, in that moment, Lucas was remembering Jon, and hearing my husband's words as he described me. Jon had always recited this, "She's hot, she's smart, and she's tough...and she's got a heart the size of Lake Superior."

Lake Superior. Yep, that's me.

I tossed my backpack over my shoulder and headed down the street.

CHAPTER TWENTY-TWO

FOR GOOD MEASURE, Kyle parked his rental in town and trekked the three miles to Samantha's house. A strange car in an established neighborhood might garner unwanted attention, the last thing he needed.

He appreciated the temperate weather, the cool breeze and dark night. The streets were virtually empty, and he caught the few sets of approaching headlights from a good distance, and ducked out of sight before they passed him by. Not like he expected a problem, and he was ready to eliminate any setbacks, should they arise, but keeping things simple was always better.

"Don't overcomplicate things. Be decisive. Get the job done." A lesson learned from Dad.

He arrived at the Stitsill home at midnight. Right on schedule. Kyle prided himself on his timeliness. His teachers had criticized him, accused him of obsessing about the clock, but they didn't understand how important time was. When he'd remind them to change class subjects at the appointed hour, they seemed aggravated with him. Dad understood though—he was proud of Kyle when he reminded him, "It's time to eat, Dad. It's time for me to go to bed." Dad appreciated him. He'd even pat him on the shoulder and say, "Good job keeping me on track, son."

By the end of the memory, Kyle was inside her house, faced with a decision. Turn on the lights, or forage around in the dark. The nearest neighbor was across the street, but lights were all extinguished there, so he felt safe turning on a few lights near the back of the Stitsill house. Thankfully, the house was shrouded by a forest of sorts, heavily wooded, and leafed out with summer's full foliage.

He decided Samantha's bedroom was where he wanted to be. He wanted to smell her. Touch her things. He wasn't a creep or anything, but he wanted to feel close to his dad. And she was the last person to have seen him alive.

He lay down on her bed and inhaled her scent. She smelled like lavender. And sweet, like clover honey. Almost like a little girl would smell. His niece, Tammy, smelled the same way and she was ten. He relaxed into the scent but soon became drowsy, a huge mistake. He hopped up from the bed and used his flashlight to rifle through her bed stand drawers. Nothing of note.

Closets were a good place to hide things. His

mom always kept things in her closet, and threatened him if he came within a foot of her bedroom door. He wasn't sure what she kept inside, but it must have been something pretty special, or seriously dangerous, the way she reared back and shook her horns at him when he came too close.

Now that he was grown, Kyle enjoyed rummaging through closets. He wasn't afraid any longer and prided himself in the fact he no longer cowered from anyone, especially women.

He went inside Samantha's closet and closed the door behind him. The tiny room had a pull-string light, which he turned on. He took a moment to breathe and relax into her smell. She had many pretty things. A feminine lady, but strong, too. Her exercise gear was proof, along with the photos on her dresser, where her beachwear unobtrusively displayed smooth biceps and finely muscled shoulders in a pic with her children.

The shelves were stacked with containers, shoeboxes, and more. Kyle knew better than to leave out any possibilities, so he methodically removed all the boxes from the shelves, being careful to keep them in order. Samantha had been thoughtful, leaving a stepstool for him, which made the process much easier and more efficient.

Along with his organizational skills, tenaciousness was another of Kyle's virtues. He found what he was searching for within forty minutes. Not as if he hunted for anything in particular, but anything related to Dad would put a grin on his face and anchor happiness in his heart.

Now, he had proof from both Detective McGrath and Samantha Stitsill. They knew his dad. They killed him, too.

Judy would believe him for once.

CHAPTER TWENTY-THREE

IN THE LIBRARY, I loaded directions from our Bar Harbor hotel to Pont-Rouge, near Quebec City, onto the screen, then pored over a popular travel site for advice. We'd be driving on route 201 most of the way. Jackman was listed as a frontier town resembling Cicely, Alaska, from the TV show, "Northern Exposure." Jon had loved the show and talked about the characters all the time, even though the series had been off the air for years. *Damn it. Jon again.*

I said a protracted prayer, asking God to help me put Jon behind me on this trip. Not so far away I forgot him all together, though. I recognized there were no clear rules for this, but in my mind, I needed to lay Jon to rest in order to commit to McGrath. I could have allowed for more shades of gray on this matter, but as long as Stitsill and his family hung over my head, all of my connections to Jon would remain strong. Or maybe I was just messed up.

I turned my attention back to the computer screen

and read about suggested restaurants along the way. I jotted down an extensive list, cautioning myself Katharine and I would have to allow time for daily long distance runs if we were going to be eating our way to Quebec.

I loaded Judith Culver's address into Google maps next, and waited with bated breath while the page loaded. I zoomed in on the house, a quaint little French affair built of fieldstone. Window boxes overflowed with flowers, and a long narrow staircase led to the front door. I wondered what I would find once I arrived on the doorstep. I needed to understand not just what I hoped to learn, but how this venture would help put meaning to mine and Jon's past.

I pulled up my recent research and reminded myself of Judith's family constellation—three sisters, a mom and dad. Stitsill had died in Japan, but maybe his ex-wife would still be alive. Maybe she'd be willing to speak with me about her husband. I wondered if her story would match Rosie's. So far, no one had anything decent to say about the guy. My own experience with the man had taught me he was a professional criminal—a ruthless killer for hire who'd wormed his way into the U.S. Government's force of contracted workers. From a personal standpoint, his history matched the underground nature of his life; he'd impregnated women and left them behind, along with his children, then went on to gather more notches on his belt. No gold stars on this guy's forehead. My gut told me if there'd been any kind of mark on his forehead, one of those women would gladly have used it as a target.

I leaned back my head and breathed in the intoxicating smell of well-read books. I told myself I didn't need to worry too much about a strict agenda for my trip. Rather, the excursion would serve as an information-gathering opportunity. I'd try to speak to Judy, maybe even share with her how I'd lost Jon and how I'd...what? Been present when her father had been shot and killed? Hit him over the head with a tire iron to be doubly sure he'd never take another breath?

Right. Good idea. What the hell is wrong with me?

Maybe I did require a plan. I needed to formulate a reasonable explanation of what I wanted from her. Something she couldn't see through. A feasible icebreaker. If I simply showed up on her doorstep, she'd be suspicious. On the other hand, I'd have the element of surprise on my side. If I were Judy, I'd invite me into her home. I'd serve a cup of tea. I'd be guarded, yet dying of curiosity about what this woman wanted. Yep. I definitely needed a plan.

I forced another deep breath of old pages, and immediately my blood pressure dropped. I had plenty of time to develop my strategy. I'd construct my plan just as I did a lesson for my students. My objective, my execution, my goal. Some polishing would be required, for sure, but mapping out my tactics made sense. Put the details within a graphic organizer in order to go into the meeting with as much preparation as possible.

I pulled up one of the plan templates I used in the classroom and proceeded to fill in a KWL chart. What I know. What I want to know. What I learned.

I filled in the first box.

WHAT I KNOW	WHAT I WANT TO KNOW	WHAT I LEARNED
• This woman called Jon thinking that he was her dad (Jon convinced her that he was not) • Judy Culver was the informant on the impostor's fake death certificate • Judy's address and Stitsill's Canada family's constellation: Wife: Barbara Daughters: Judy-44, Marlowe-41, Rachel-40	• Was Judy's image in the photo of Rosie's wedding? • What did Judy and her siblings know about their dad? • Had the impostor (their dad) always been a scoundrel? • What did they know about him? • When did they last see him? • Why did Judy think Jon was her father? • How long ago had they seen their father alive? • Did they know their father had been in the Peace Corps at one time? • Did they know of a relationship between their dad and my late husband?	• Nothing yet

I spent several long moments mulling over my template. It was the perfect place to start. I could add to the document whenever a new thought popped up, plus I'd have all the information in one spot, ready and waiting.

Now for the execution. I scratched my head. I could watch her home. Wait for her to leave. See where she went. Was that kind of behavior considered surveillance or stalking?

I opted for my original idea. I'd show up on her doorstep. Since I didn't look threatening, I guessed she'd open the door for me. I'd explain who I was and what I hoped to discover—how my husband and her dad were related. The prospect of the conversation caused my pulse to quicken. I'd begun jiggling my knee, and my fingers thrummed against my thigh.

I hunched over the screen and searched for a hotel. A Fairmont popped up. Vacancy. Spectacular views. On a bluff overlooking the St. Lawrence River, the lodgings appeared to be quite romantic— best described as a castle. Or maybe, a palace. With any luck, such decadence wouldn't cause Katharine and me to miss our men. Or, maybe, if we did, we'd invite them to join us. Food for thought.

Judy's house was located thirty minutes from the hotel. I booked five nights, from Monday to Friday, thinking if we wrapped things up in less time, we could shorten our stay. Plus, if I wanted to visit with Judy, the Fairmont would be the perfect place to leave Katharine. Plenty of shopping and historical venues to visit. I'd pull the funds out of the life insurance trust fund Jon left behind. I tried not to touch the money, to live simply from my salary, and save the kids' college trust fund for emergencies, but I knew how much I could pull from my stash without causing the world to shift, and this seemed a fitting investment—finding out more about my late husband and his impostor.

I had a plan.

I shut down and tucked my laptop inside my backpack, and practically skipped down the short staircase and out onto the sidewalk. My smile stayed with me the length of the block, and deepened when I spotted McGrath standing by the car, his head in the trunk and his fine derriere meeting my gaze.

He swung around when he heard me approach. "Hey," he said, and gave me an approving nod.

"What?" I asked.

"You look amazing."

"How is that possible? I'm a sweaty mess." I reached up and smoothed my hair, loose ends tumbling from my ponytail, and felt a sudden twinge of sadness. I'd miss him next week when I was in Quebec. I suffered a pang of guilt as well, for not divulging the true intentions for my trip.

We decided on a quick stop back to the hotel for my shower, or perhaps a mutual shower, then a long trek in the mountains. The temperature had climbed to the mid-seventies already, a perfect day for a hike. I shared the travel itinerary for the following week with him. Katharine and I would leave Monday morning and return Friday in time for date night. If I got hung up in Quebec and needed to stay the fifth night, I could formulate some last minute excuse on the fly: car trouble, one more sightseeing adventure, too tired to drive. Easy peasy.

***

Color me weird, but I could hardly contain myself I was so excited. The steep climb up the mountain left McGrath winded. On the other hand, I could have scaled a few hundred feet more. How he could worry that I'd miss teaching in favor of doing investigative work was beyond me. I was high on mystery.

"If I didn't know better, I'd say you were on drugs," he said.

I tossed my hair off my shoulder. "Just having a fabulous day. The sun is shining. The birds are singing. The air is fresh. We're on vacation."

McGrath narrowed his eyes and studied me.

His gaze bore into me—I was in a fishbowl where the glass magnified each and every cell of my being. If I could have, I'd have run for cover. As McGrath's memory improved, so did his skills. *Damn.* What if he saw right through me?

"I've seen you like this before," he said. "Just can't remember when."

"Life is going our way," I explained. "You're

recovering your memory. We're ready to plan our future. I'm loving the opportunity to spend time on me."

McGrath cocked his head. "It's not an indictment. I'm just noticing."

I still felt transparent and worried that if I so much as blinked, he'd see right through me. Discover my hidden agenda. All the air gusted out of me. What was I doing? Pursuing some crazy lead, which had attached itself to me like Velcro. Why?

I needed a keeper. Or a straight jacket.

This was plain old silly. A bad idea. I'd experienced plenty of closure in the two years since Jon's death. If I didn't let go of this ridiculous notion, I should consider signing up at the nearest sanitarium on my way home.

Then again, the time away would provide Katharine and I the opportunity to cement our friendship, afford her some much needed time away from Paul, and grant me the chance to pursue the real story of hers and Ben's relationship. Not knowing ate at me like a festering sore.

I convinced myself, stopping off and meeting Stitsill's daughter Judy was an added treat to an already full trip. So there.

CHAPTER TWENTY-FOUR

PACKED AND READY to go, I loaded my bag in the trunk and searched for the directions to Katharine's home. Since she planned to drive, McGrath agreed to drop me at her place on his way to teach at the museum. We'd spent time making sure we had each other's bodies memorized the night before, and the moonstruck glow still hung in my smile.

McGrath sauntered up behind me and pressed his lips to my neck. "I'm going to miss you," he said, his arms encircling my waist.

"Last night was amazing. I love rocket beds."

He gazed at me wistfully. "Great trip to outer space."

"I'll be back before you know it." I leaned back my head and kissed his whiskered cheek. "Plus, you won't have to shave for five days. You'll be in heaven."

"There's that." He gave me a squeeze before letting go.

"Je t'aime," I said, flexing my French muscle.

"I have no idea what you just said, but back at ' ya."

"Glad you trust me to say only nice things." I winked at him before climbing into the passenger seat.

We arrived at Katharine's on the stroke of nine. She stood on the front walk, waving, as we pulled in front of the house.

"You've got your cell phone, right?" McGrath asked.

"You're a worry wart," I said. "I'll be fine."

"Separation anxiety," he admitted.

I grabbed his inner thigh and squeezed. "I promise. I'm coming back."

He planted his lips on mine and my body briefly relived the previous night, an aftershock from last night's love quake jolted my middle.

Katharine's voice rang out. "Hey, you two lovebirds, give it a rest."

I patted McGrath's knee and separated myself from his embrace.

"Ok. We're off," I said.

He transferred my bag from our trunk to the back of Katharine's SUV as I gave her a quick hug. "Is Paul inside?" I asked. "I want to say hello."

"In the kitchen," she said, then called out to McGrath, "Help me with my bag?"

I announced myself as I entered the front room. He answered from the kitchen, where he sat hunched over his computer, fingers racing over the keys. I stood and waited while he finished.

"You look like you're in the middle of something," I said.

"An article for the Times on the diagnosis of ADHD in adolescents." He studied me, a serious expression on his face.

"Thanks for letting me abscond with your wife for a few days."

"I'm sure the two of you will have a great time." His tone was morose, which made me think back to the rainy-day discussion Katharine and I had. It would be tough to live with someone whose mood swung like the pendulum on a grandfather clock. He'd seemed so upbeat the night we spent with them last week, but his disposition had soured. Maybe he was wrapped up in his article.

"I'll take good care of your woman. And Jim will be around if you get lonely."

"I've been alone before."

Ok, definitely not just work on his mind.

I leaned over and placed a quick peck on his cheek. "See you Friday." I left him and high-tailed my way out the front door.

I said another goodbye to McGrath, whispering he might want to check on Paul mid-week, figuring he could lighten his surliness with a shared beer. McGrath waved as we pulled away.

Katharine had plugged our destination into her

GPS and she headed to US-1 S.

"Beautiful day for a drive," I mused.

She stayed quiet. I guessed she and Paul had words very different from the ones McGrath and I had shared before our departure.

"You okay?" I asked.

"I will be. Just need a minute."

"Music?" I pulled out my iPhone and Bluetoothed my device to her car. Then I tuned in "Baby Got Back." Even though the song was outdated, my kids played Sir Mix-a-Lot when my mood fell into the pits, and the words always cheered me up. I hoped the lyrics would make Katharine smile.

Within seconds, her frown disappeared. Soon, she giggled. "That's the funniest song. Thanks."

"I got your back, girlfriend."

An hour later, we crossed the border into Canada without a hitch. Showing my passport conjured up memories of Jon's stolen identity. The late night phone calls, the woman who claimed she was married to a man with my husband's exact vital statistics. My dog's death. My husband's death. Meeting my husband's killer in Japan of all places, and mine and McGrath's ensuing confrontation with a real-life assassin. I'd never look at my passport in the same way again. My heart would always catch in my chest. I shifted in the passenger's seat, facing the new reality, and made a conscious effort to block out the accompanying sorrow.

We spent the next two hours talking about cases at work and about the challenges teachers faced now as opposed to twenty years previous, before we made a pit stop for coffee. Once we were driving again, Katharine glanced over at me.

"Why are we really heading to Quebec?" she asked.

"I'm translucent?"

"Consider me a skilled practitioner."

"Some of my husband's family lives there. Family I've never met." I'd stretched the truth, but total honesty seemed like a bad decision.

"Are you sure you want to beat a dead horse?" She caught herself a moment too late. "Ugh. Sorry. How insensitive of me."

"I'm curious…and," I confessed, "closure eludes me."

"Closure is overrated," she said. "Why don't you tell me what's tying up your brain?"

And so I did.

"I come so close to giving myself over to Jim— God knows when I'm with him I rarely think of Jon. But for some reason, when I think about marrying the man, something stops me."

"Could be his amnesia, plus, he's unemployed, and his hotness isn't quite enough reassurance for a long term commitment."

"He's a wonderful man. He's devoted to me and

the kids."

"Dogs are devoted and nice. You could get a dog."

She really was in a mood.

"I had a dog. McGrath's better than a dog."

"Well, we have that settled. What about the whole job thing? Do you mind supporting him?"

I sensed this question came from a deeper place. Maybe Paul's books weren't selling as well as he'd indicated. I'd never heard of him before. Maybe he was one of those authors who still struggled for every dime. Then again, he had said he was writing an article for the *Times*.

"Well?" Katharine's voice nudged me from my thoughts.

"He's been on paid leave from the detective force since his accident. Not a boatload of money, and he's only six months away from a more permanent decision. Maybe you're right. Maybe the uncertainty is bothering me. I don't normally have time to think about these things. I'm busy when I'm home. But in a traditional relationship work might be a looming factor."

"It would bother me."

"Money isn't a huge factor for me. What I really worry about," I paused, unsure I wanted to say the words aloud.

"What?" Her voice became softer. Gentler.

I clenched my jaw. "I worry he'll change if his

memory returns. He'll change his mind about me."

"Never going to happen. You're being silly."

"Maybe."

"What's making you so insecure?"

"You're right. I'm being ridiculous. It's weird though. I put a lot on him. I want his memory to return. I want him to be whole again. He's quite content though."

"You need to relax."

"You're right, I do. He's remembered parts of his past since we've been here. The doctors said years might go by before he remembered. They also said he might never remember. I keep thinking I'll be able to jog his memory."

"Not your job. And if he's recalling more, it might make sense to let things take their natural course rather than try to force him."

I bit the inside of my cheek. "I'm one of those people who likes to think I have far more control than I actually do."

"Take a break the next few days, huh?"

"You, too," I said.

"Agreed." Katharine turned up the volume on the radio and we sang along to "Teenage Dream," rolling down the windows and letting our hair blow in the wind.

We stopped for lunch, jogged around a rest stop a couple of hours later to loosen the kinks, and traded spots once we climbed back into the car. Two hours later, I drove across the LaPorte Bridge, crossing the St-Laurent River. The city opened up below, decidedly European, like a travelogue—neutral brick buildings with brightly painted entrances, overflowing planters on second story windows, and cobblestone streets full of tourists and residents.

We pulled into the Fairmont Le Chateau Frontenac parking lot by 4 A.M. Perched high on a bluff overlooking the river, the hotel dominated the metropolis, resembling something from a fairy tale. I was Cinderella, just arriving at the ball. Only I'd arrived in a Ford Explorer rather than a magic coach. And I'd opted for a pair of khaki pants and a blouse rather than a ball gown. And I'd left my prince behind. Small matters.

The day still young, we dropped our bags inside our room before wandering the expansive, luxurious grounds. I spotted a lap pool on our tour and vowed to rise early and swim before starting out the following day.

We located a pleasant pub on a nearby cobblestone street and settled in with cold beers and a bowl of peanuts.

"I'm going to be straight with you," I said.

"Shoot."

"I'm here to do some research on this family. There are secrets on Jon's side. I'm here to unearth them."

"You've got my attention."

"I have reason to believe this side of Jon's family has ties to him they never wanted him to know about." I twisted the story, concocted a believable tale, and one less scary than the truth. I offered Katharine slivers of reality. This way, I could justify disappearing for a few hours each day to conduct my research.

"Like what?"

"I think my husband may have been named after a gentleman from Quebec. I'm not sure why, but his kids reached out to my Jon, hoping he knew something about their father. The matching surname first prompted them to get in touch, but nothing much came of the contact because Jon traveled and didn't have time to spend embroiled in this family's drama."

Katharine arched her brows. "But you're a sucker for drama, and your life has been free of major crisis since Jim's accident."

"Pretty much sums me up."

"Count me in."

"What?"

"You were married to a guy who was never home. You have questions. You want to meet these people and find out how they're connected to your husband. I'm on board."

"I'm not sure I understand." I sipped my beer, hoping to calm the jitters.

"I love soap operas, and there aren't many on TV any more. Let's create our own."

"Wouldn't you rather schedule a massage at the spa, go shopping, have a manicure?"

"Nope." Katharine locked eyes with me.

"Skeletons and closets, Katharine. Might be dangerous."

She raised her glass to mine. "Thelma and Louise, honey. You remember them, right?"

"I watched them on cable."

"You and me, girlfriend. You and me."

She raised her mug to mine. "Cheers."

CHAPTER TWENTY-FIVE

I FELT CONSPIRATORIAL. Or manipulative. I hadn't shared everything I knew with Katharine. And I worried. I'd almost put Di's well-being in jeopardy when I first became involved with Rosita Stitsill and the whole mystery surrounding the theft of Jon's identity. By forcing McGrath to help me track down the details of Jon's death, I'd almost cost him his life. Why couldn't I leave well enough alone? I didn't want to risk putting Katharine's life in danger.

Calm down, Samantha. You're getting ahead of yourself.

I was simply visiting a long-lost member of Jon's family. Check that. Jon's killer's family. My heart skipped a beat. Maybe two.

I tossed and turned like the princess with a pea under her mattress, finally falling asleep two hours before dawn. I awakened groggy and out of sorts. Katharine, on the other hand, stretched and smiled as she opened her eyes.

"When do we leave?" she asked.

Her excitement gave me a lift. "Shall we exercise first?"

She trotted over to the Keurig machine and made us each a cup of coffee. "Let's skip our run today. I'm anxious to tackle this mystery."

"I'm having second thoughts about involving you."

"Look at things this way," Katharine said, her mind made up. "I'm a grown woman, capable of making my own decisions. Plus, I'm a psychologist. I can help you."

I mulled over her words. She had two valid points.

I tossed my legs over the side of the bed. "We should have a hearty breakfast first."

"Right after we shower."

"Deal," I said.

We took turns getting ready, then discussed my approach with Judy, Stitsill's daughter, over breakfast.

"I'm going to be direct," I said. "Remind her of her call to Jon years ago, and explain I'm trying to tie up loose ends. Tell her Jon died two years ago. Play on her sympathies a little, and give her as little information as possible. Beef up the possibility of a connection."

"What are you hoping to discover?"

"I want to know more about her father," I said, slurping down some fresh-squeezed orange juice.

"Specifically?"

"It's complicated. I have reason to believe he came from a long line of thugs. I have this sneaky suspicion he may be related to Alfred de Marigny."

"Wait." Katharine laid her hand on my wrist. "The guy who was suspected of killing Sir Harry Oakes?"

"You know about him?"

"Honey, I've lived in Bar Harbor my entire life. Everyone knows the story."

"I know this sounds preposterous, but I discovered some sketchy links. I've also looked at photos and the Marigny guy looks a lot like Judy's father. I think Marigny might have been her grandfather."

"Wow," Katharine said. "Truth is stranger than fiction."

"We'll find out."

"Do you think we should call her first?"

"I can't decide," I admitted. "Part of me feels like showing up at her front door so she doesn't have the chance to shut me down. If I call first, she may decide she doesn't want to talk to me."

"Makes sense. But she could turn us away if we show up unannounced."

"This is what I'm banking on," I said. "When Judy called Jon years ago, she seemed desperate to reach her father. Somehow, she and her dad had lost touch over the years. In fact," I admitted, "I had a sneaking suspicion she suspected Jon was her father."

"Did she really?"

"I'm not sure." I sank back in my chair, taking in my surroundings. The dining room was exquisite—a huge carved fireplace, an ornate French provincial chandelier, gilded upholstered chairs, and linen tablecloths. All of this seemed in sharp contrast to what I was about to do. Dig up dirt.

I shook off the anxiety.

"Let's take flowers. Women love flowers." Katharine popped a strawberry into her mouth, and sat forward, satisfaction in her eyes. "Come on. We can do this."

"You're right. Let's walk down the street and find a flower shop." I checked my watch. "Judy's home is fifteen minutes away. We can plug her address into your GPS. If we take time to stop and grab a bouquet, we'll arrive at a presentable time."

"Want to rehearse?"

I eyed her with added respect. "God, you're good."

"Cheap entertainment," she said. "This is going to be fun!"

If this was going to be so much damned fun, why was my leg trembling under the table? I signaled the waiter for our tab, signed the charge to our room, and we headed out.

Katharine assumed the lead and marched up to the hostess stand where she inquired about a florist. Then, she gripped my arm and led me out of the hotel.

"This way," she said, turning left.

We made our way down a narrow street, easily found the florist, purchased an incredible bunch of violet hydrangeas, and hurried to the car.

I wanted to drive. I needed to drive.

Katharine took one look at me and handed over the keys.

God, I loved this woman.

We pulled up in front of Judy Stitsill Culver's home as the dashboard clock display read 10 A.M. The white Camry parked in the drive indicated someone was inside. I breathed a sigh of relief, but my heart didn't stop racing. It rammed against my ribs double-time.

Katharine gathered the bouquet in her arms. She wore a huge grin, like a kid who'd just been released from school at the final bell.

"What are you so happy about?" I whispered.

Katharine elbowed me. "Get your act together, Sam. We have to look the part."

She had a valid point. I pasted a grin on my face and rang the bell. I willed my drumming heart to slow, and was almost successful, until I heard the deadbolt fall on the other side of the door. Sure as Shinola, Judy Stitsill opened the door. I recognized her from the wedding photo Rosita had shown me a few years ago. Taller than I expected, she'd maintained her figure. Her blonde hair, drawn back into a ponytail, made her steel blue eyes jump out from a soft oval face. She had a definite girl-next-door look. Her puzzled expression led me to think I'd better talk fast, and not allow her the chance to slam the door in my face.

"Hi, I'm Samantha Stitsill. From the States. You called my house and talked to my husband a long time ago. You were trying to reach your dad. I don't know if you remember or not, but my husband shared your father's name." *And a few other vital statistics, for that matter.* I waited for some acknowledgment.

Recognition flashed in her eyes as she shifted from one foot to the other, as if deciding what to do. "You've come all this way to see me?"

"My friend Katharine and I have always wanted to see Quebec," I lied. "And on the drive up, I remembered you lived here." She hadn't told Jon she lived in Quebec. She'd said Canada. Would she see through my lie? Would she boot me for trying to deceive her or be intrigued by it? Too late now.

She narrowed her eyes, seemingly weighing her options. "I was just about to leave for the gym."

Seemed right. She wore the usual outfit—stretchy pants and a sleeveless workout shirt with the words "Train insane or remain the same." Not my style, but whatever.

Katharine leaned in. "Since you and Sam are probably relatives, we hated to come without a gift. Hope you enjoy these." She handed over the bouquet.

"We understand about exercise. The two of us are maniacs. We can touch base later, or some other time altogether. No worries."

"Don't be silly." Judy warmed up. "I can head to the gym later. It's just a spin class. It kicks my ass. For once, I have a valid reason to miss. Out of town relatives. The perfect excuse." She grinned and opened the screen door, waving us inside.

She said *relatives*. Trepidation replaced my elation. I'm a good person, I know. But I *had* walloped Judy's father over the head with a tire iron in Japan. Just to make certain he was dead. I hadn't actually killed him, yet part of me felt I had. I'd certainly wished him dead. And had I the chance to take him out before McGrath did, I would have delivered the fatal shot without flinching.

Did Judy realize any of this? Did she know her father was deceased? What did she know about her dad?

That's what I planned to find out. *Carry on, Sam. Worry about the details later.*

I marched inside, right behind Katharine, who seemed to enjoy her role more than I would have guessed. Like nobody's business, she made small talk with Judy. "What a lovely home. Have you been here long? It's so fresh and quaint."

"Four years," Judy answered. "My husband and I refurbished the place before we moved in. We refinished the cove moldings and patched the plaster ourselves, rather than updating to dry wall and new woodwork. We love the charm of the place. It's a hundred years old."

Jon and I had done the same to our place. In that moment, I hated knowing Judy and I had things in common. I'd been prepared to dislike her.

She led us into a lovely living room, filled with antique furniture, Tiffany lamps, and Renaissance-era prints. Tapestry curtains hung heavy over the windows. Ornate, yet comfortable. "What can I get you? Coffee? Tea? A cold drink?"

Shit. She was warm and friendly, too.

"I'd love a cup of tea. Sam?" Katharine fired a snap-out-of-it look at me.

"Tea. Yes."

Judy scurried off to the kitchen while Katharine settled herself on the velvet-covered Queen Anne sofa, posing like the queen herself. Legs crossed at the ankles, hands neatly folded in her lap. She hissed at me. "Sam!"

"What?" I inventoried the book titles on the built-in shelves. Classics. All classics. This encouraged me. Her mind didn't work like mine— constantly investigating even when a mystery didn't exist. Maybe she wouldn't suspect my motivation after all. Then I searched for photos of her dad, or Rosita, any signs that they were close.

"Are you alright?"

Good question. "Sure. Just deciding where to

head with our conversation."

I sat in a delicate chair near the sofa, but assumed a stance I'd seen McGrath adopt on more than one occasion. I leaned forward, elbows rested on my knees, chin propped by my fists. Thinking. Thinking. How would I do this? I should've rehearsed as Katharine had suggested last night.

Katharine left me to my thoughts. I scrambled for a few minutes, the pot whistling in the kitchen snapping me back to reality. I had mere moments. I decided to do what I do best. Jump head first, off the cliff.

Judy appeared with a silver tray, china teapot, and cups. We were getting the royal treatment. She set the tea service on the coffee table.

"I lost my husband two years ago," I said.

Judy's eyes shared a look of sadness. "My dad died, too."

Don't I know it. "I'm so sorry, I had no idea." *Did I just say that?* "Was he ill?" I'd used that same line with Rosita when she visited me at parent-teacher conferences and shared details about her husband, Judy's father.

She poured the tea and handed me a cup. "We'd been estranged for many years. Still, word of his death hit me hard."

I took a sip of tea and posed sympathetically. Katharine faded into the background, busying herself with a thorough examination of her teacup and its contents.

"It's been quite a while since you spoke with my husband. Were you able to locate your dad?"

"He sent me a letter from Botswana, but long before I tried to reach him in the States."

Wait. *Wait a damned minute*! This didn't add up. She'd been in her father's wedding photos. I'd seen them with my own eyes. And I'd seen her name on her dad's death certificate. None of this made sense. My mind whirred like my kids'Frisbee.

I put the events in place. She tried to reach her dad before I'd met Rosita, Judy's stepmother. That made sense. But he had married Rosita after his return from Botswana. I knew this for a fact. I crunched more numbers. Eleven years ago, he died, but in reality he faked his death. This was a few years after he'd married Rosita. I had yet to determine the reason, but assumed he needed to disappear because Rosita was on to him. She suspected his actual profession was hired gun. He was committed to a career that didn't lend itself to a full-time family.

In my mind, he faked his death because he needed to disappear. But so many other questions filled my head. How had Judy become a Stitsill? Had her father changed his name? Then the names of his children? Why adopt my husband's identity? Was it mere chance—or something more? My back began to spasm. My head began to throb. I needed time to think, but I had none.

What did I come here for? Oh, right. To establish a possible link between Alfred de Marigny and Jon Stitsill, my husband's impostor.

Solve the main question first, Sam. The easiest.

I ignored her comments about her dad's letter and focused on my present mission. "My husband often wondered if there was a link to the Marigny family. His mother had done some work on the family tree years ago, and thought there might be a connection."

Grains of truth. What did it really matter if there were a link between the Marigny's and the impostor? Except to prove that he had con man, murderer, and thief in his DNA.

Judy sipped her tea and smiled. "Alfred de Marigny was my grandfather."

My heartbeat paused for a full sixty seconds.

"Wow!" was all I could say. "I've read about him. That's why I was interested."

"Everyone is. The case against my grandfather was dismissed almost seventy years ago, you know. He was acquitted. He didn't murder Sir Harry. Ancient history."

"My mother-in-law loved soap operas. The Marigny name was on her husband's side, so the melodrama appealed to her," I lied. "My husband never thought much of it. So, how did your dad wind up with the surname Stitsill?"

"He'd always been ashamed of his dad. Alfred returned to Quebec after the trial, but was deported three years later. He lived in the States, Jamaica, and Haiti before finally settling in Central America. My grandmother returned to Quebec after my dad was born. She'd divorced Alfred by then. After she died, twelve years ago, Dad decided to make the change. He legally changed his name to Stitsill, and we followed suit."

Incredible.

"Was Stitsill a family name from your mother's side?"

"I'm not sure how he decided on the name. Dad made impulsive decisions about things I'd have given more thought to, but we were accustomed to his impetuous verdicts. When he decided to live in the States, we wondered why, but tossed the move off to Dad being Dad."

"I don't mean to pry, but did he and your mom divorce?"

"When I was sixteen." A sadness enveloped her.

"I'm sorry."

Katharine broke in. "Divorce is tough on teenagers."

"How long ago did he change his name? Weren't you an adult? I know I seem snoopy, but it's curious you decided to change your name as well."

Judy shifted in her chair. "Eleven years ago. I'd just turned twenty-nine. As a single girl with no prospects, I hoped to reconnect with my dad. Normal stuff for a girl that age, I suspect."

"Girls need their dads," Katharine interjected.

"I'd always wanted more than Dad was able to provide." Judy went on. "I thought if I changed my name, he might pay more attention. Not just to me, but my siblings. He pulled away from us when he divorced Mom. I hoped if I gave him the chance, he'd come back."

While the timeline matched what I knew about my husband's impostor, the facts seemed preposterous. An idea dawned on me. Jon's passport had been stolen in Toronto. Stitsill could have purchased and assumed his new identity anywhere. In Canada or in the States. And if he worked undercover as a hired gun for the U.S., my own government could have arranged for him to assume my husband's identity.

I couldn't think of another avenue to pursue. I should have planned ahead. *Damn my impulsivity.* "I guess this means we aren't related after all." I tried to sound disappointed, then glanced at my watch. "We've kept you too long. I'm sorry for the intrusion."

I glanced at Katharine, who looked puzzled.

"It's been lovely meeting you," Judy said. "How long will you be in Quebec?"

"Five days."

"You should treat yourself at L'Initiale while you're here. It's expensive, but the food is divine."

I desperately wanted to leave the door open to another meeting or phone call, but I couldn't think of one darn reason that made sense. *Your dad killed his wife. Your step-siblings are living with my best friend. Your dad left a million dollars behind.*

The last one might interest her. I took in my surroundings once again. I had no idea of the cost of real estate in Quebec, but this home stood in an old neighborhood of well-kept homes. Not mansions, mind you, but nicer homes. I made a mental note to research this, noting that she didn't appear wealthy, but neither was she in dire straits.

"You should join us for lunch one day," I said. "Even though we're not blood relatives, we share the same name."

Judy bit her bottom lip. "I'm not sure of my schedule. Once you decide on a day, give me a call." She paused and jotted her phone number on a post-it note.

Perfect.

CHAPTER TWENTY-SIX

WE SAID A pleasant goodbye to Judy, each sharing a comfortable embrace with her. My mind, riddled with questions and confusion, wouldn't settle down. I let Katharine drive back to the hotel, which earned me a concerned gaze.

I stood at a crossroads. I desperately wanted to talk this through. Out loud. But not with her. I was in way over my head. Again. *Crap.*

I considered calling McGrath, but what good would that do? I kicked myself. I should have shared the underlying reason for my trip with him. But I knew what the outcome would have been. He would have stopped me from coming to Quebec.

An idea came to me. Call Lucas Sweeney. He'd appreciate knowing more about the history of this family. After all, he'd witnessed Stitsill murder an innocent man. He'd known Rosie. He'd known my Jon. And he'd been there when McGrath had killed Judy's father. He'll talk this through with me.

I thought about my conversation with Judy.

There had to be more. Not like it would amount to anything, but if I'd been an international spy as I suspected Lucas Sweeney to be, I'd have liked to tidy up matters around a man whom I'd spent years hunting.

I vowed to phone Lucas as soon as I stole a few minutes away from Katharine. Not like I didn't already know what he would say. *Let it go, Sam. It doesn't matter.* He tolerated me. Even felt responsible for me because of his relationship with Jon. I knew he felt he should have prevented Jon's death. We didn't talk often, but I was sure he kept an eye on me. From a distance.

Katharine cleared her throat, jolting me back to reality. "What do you think?"

"I'm not sure."

"She seems nice. I think we could be friends with her."

Sounded a little over the top to me. Unnecessary, even.

"A little too close to home, if you catch my drift."

Katharine flicked off the radio. "Are you ever going to tell me?"

"Tell you what?"

"About your husband. About the connections to Judy. What are you really sorting out?"

Good question. I couldn't tell her everything, but I didn't need to keep everything to myself. What stuck in my head most was the phone call. I'd called Jon in Japan, shortly before his death, and a woman had answered the phone. Not housekeeping. A woman. I had buried those memories along with my husband, but they had a way of creeping in now and then. And now, more than ever. A slew of memories flashed before me. Times when Jon had to take a call. Times when he would glance at a text message, then disappear from sight a few moments later. My antenna had shot up, but I'd chosen to deny my suspicions. I needed Jon. I needed to believe in him. Believe I was his one and only.

Although the impostor, the man responsible for my husband's death had confessed that he set Jon up and made it look like he was having an affair, I wondered now. Was he? After all this time, did it really matter? Like it or not, I would never really know. I had decided to shelve the memory a long time ago. Why was I pulling it down now?

Seeing Judy had resurrected too much. Enough. Time to settle in to my real life, and let go of the past. *Go ahead, Sam. Lie to yourself. That'll work!*

"You caught me. I'm reminiscing."

"Let's play a game," Katharine said.

"Okay, great. I love games."

"Sarcasm doesn't suit you, Sam."

"Sorry. Go ahead. Really. What do you want to play?"

"I ask you a question. You have to answer

honestly. Then you get to ask me one. And I'll answer. Honestly."

I winked at her. "Deal."

"What are you afraid of?"

"Snakes. And spiders."

She guffawed. "If you're not going to be straight with me, I'll never play with you again. Now, I'll ask again. What are you really afraid of?"

"Alright, alright. Giving myself to someone."

She passed me a sideways glance and merged onto the freeway. "You mean a man, right?"

"Exactly." I gazed out the window. "This conversation would be better served over a drink."

Katharine tapped the GPS touch screen. "There's a pub at the next exit."

"Perfect." *What was I afraid of? And why did I keep making excuses? McGrath. Amnesia. All good reasons. But if he didn't have amnesia, would I have signed up then?*

By the time I checked back in, Katharine was pulling into a parking place at Bull's Bistro. "Fitting, don't you agree? The way I see things, you're not allowed to bullshit me here. The bull's already taken."

I snorted, itched my nose, and decided I might admit a few things to Katharine, and maybe even admit a few things to myself in the process.

We tucked ourselves into a table in the back.

I frowned. "Too bad I can't smoke in here."

"You don't smoke, do you?"

"No, but if I did … this would be a good time."

"Try courage in liquid form. I highly recommend a craft brew. Canadians know beer. Drinking is much easier on your lungs than cigarettes."

Luckily, Katharine spoke enough French to order us each a micro-brew and we settled in at the neighborhood bar. Once my Belgian ale arrived, I sipped. Cool, bubbly, delicious.

She studied me. "So, you don't want to let a man in."

"I want to, but I'm not sure I know how."

"Did you let your husband in?"

"Yes. Absolutely." I drooped against the slats of the chair. "No. Maybe not."

Katharine nodded. "Mmmhmm."

I wagged a finger at her. "No psychologist-type murmurings. Part of the rules."

"Sorry," she said. "Lapse of judgment."

"I know all the reasons. I'm afraid of getting hurt, don't want to rely on someone else, not worth the risk of losing someone. But my trepidation runs far deeper. I make excuses for myself all the time. In Jon's case, he left so frequently that I told myself life would be easier if I didn't come to depend on him. In the case of McGrath, I have come so very close to leaning on him. But I'm afraid of losing myself if I truly give myself to someone else. Wait. Maybe that's not what I'm afraid of at all. Maybe what I'm truly afraid of is...finding myself."

"Interesting proposition. How does anyone figure that out?"

I arched my brows. "You're the psychologist." I took a gulp of my beer this time. "In essence, I know myself pretty well, but I'm afraid if I—shit. I have no idea."

Katharine swallowed hard. "Me neither."

I softened my voice and leaned forward. "Tell me about Ben."

"Love of my life. But I'm with Paul now."

"Happily?"

"You know we're not happy. We're married though. Committed."

"Is Ben with anyone? Do you think you still have a chance?"

"I have no idea. But I could never leave Paul. He needs me. He's so depressed … I can't imagine what would happen to him."

"But that's on him, not you."

"And what if he killed himself, Sam? Are you saying I'd be okay living with the guilt? Knowing I was responsible?"

"You're right. I'd like to make life simple, but it's not. Nothing is. Think about this, I'm two years out from Jon's death and there are still things that trouble me. Unanswered questions."

"Like the link to Judy and her family?"

"No, like the fact that a woman answered his phone when I called him in Japan a few days before he died."

"Oh, no. I'm so sorry."

"I haven't thought about these plaguing questions or talked about them in so long. Why is this coming at me now?"

"Maybe because Jim's memory is returning. You're a packaging person, am I right? Neat little boxes suit you better than messy piles."

I studied her. She'd figured me out pretty damn quick. "I'm as transparent as plate glass. Crap."

"You have to learn to let go, Sam. Not like I'm one to talk, but it's all right to move on. If your husband was having an affair, it's ancient history."

"It makes me question who I am though. I was lonely, too. Would I have had an affair if he hadn't died?"

"Are you trying to let Jon off the hook?"

"Maybe. I feel like I'm circling the drain here. Let's get back to you."

Katharine picked up her mug and drained her beer. "We're not so different, Sam."

"How do you mean?"

"I'm staying with Paul because I can't handle the long-term guilt I'd suffer by leaving him, and you're holding onto Jon in the same way."

"Because I feel guilty?"

She laid her hand atop mine.

"Seems so."

CHAPTER TWENTY-SEVEN

I ENCOURAGED KATHARINE to go for a run without me. I feigned a headache and the need for an extra thirty minutes of sleep. I phoned Lucas as soon as she shut the door behind her.

"Hi, Sam."

"Lucas, I'm in Quebec City. I've been to Judy Stitsill's home and she's related to Alfred de Marigny. In fact, he was Stitsill's father. Do you know who he is?"

"The name sounds familiar but I can't place it. Who is he?"

I relayed the entire story.

"So what are you saying? That a bad guy—a dead bad guy—is related to another dead bad guy."

"When you put it like that, it sounds stupid."

"I don't mean to minimize your findings, but really, Sam…What are you doing?"

All the air rushed out of me, and even though I was still lying in bed, I felt dizzy, and nauseous.

"You have to let go of this. For your own sanity."

My cell signaled another call. "I have another call, Lucas. Thanks for listening. You're right. I need to let this go."

"Take care, Sam."

I answered the other call, paying no attention to the caller ID.

"Samantha?"

"Yes?"

"This is Judy Culver. You and your friend Katharine visited my home yesterday."

I sat up. "Oh, yes. Hi."

"I enjoyed our visit, and I would love to have the chance to meet again. You caught me by surprise when you stopped by, and I'm afraid I was reticent to share some facts with you." *Right. You out and out lied to me.* "But, now I've had time to think, and—if you could find time..."

Sure, I'll take more.

"We're busy today, when are you thinking?" I needed processing time, and time to decide on my approach with Katharine. Some things Judy might choose to share might cause Katharine to question her choice of friends.

"I was hoping sometime soon. I know you aren't here for long, and I hate to interrupt your vacation, but you mentioned getting together again. I'm sure you suggested another meeting as a matter of courtesy, but, if I'm not stepping out of line, I feel so connected to you, as if you could be a friend."

Now, she sounded as manipulative as her dad. Even if she hadn't spent a lot of time with him growing up, she'd inherited his ability to use charm as bait for a mighty catch.

"I'll check with Katharine and get back to you. Can I let you know in an hour or so?"

"Perfect."

I disconnected the call, a knot tightening in my gut. The two of us were poised, bouncing on our toes in either corner of the ring. I hadn't a clue what she hoped to snake out of me, but I was determined to steal some treasures of my own.

Katharine bobbed through the door thirty minutes later, sweaty but charged with the adrenalin rush of a good, solid run.

"How far did you go?"

She checked her Garmin. "Eight miles."

"You're incredible. I couldn't run eight if a tiger was chasing me."

"Sure you could. You're the mistress of underestimation. You never give yourself enough credit."

"We can challenge my inadequacies tomorrow morning, right before we return to Judy Culver's house."

"What?"

"She called. Seems she'd like to be our new BFF."

Katharine rubbed her hands together as if she'd

just discovered a magic potion.

"Great news. What more do you want to get out of her?"

She plopped down on the edge of the bed as I propped a pillow behind my head and sat forward to fill her in. "I think the time has come for me to be straight with you."

"You think?"

I drew my lips into a thin line. She had a tongue as sharp as mine. "I've been trying to protect you."

She pursed her lips. "For my own good, I'm sure."

"Judy was lying when we met with her yesterday. She said the last she heard from her dad was when he was in Botswana, but in truth, I have copies of photos taken from her Dad's wedding to Rosita, a Hispanic woman who accused me of being married to her husband—"

"Slow down. Start at the beginning."

"I don't know if I can do a *Reader's Digest* version, but I'll try. Judy's dad stole my husband's identity. He remarried, to Rosie, on his return from Botswana, where he posed as a Peace Corp worker. They had a child together, and he committed suicide when the baby was almost two."

Katharine's eyes widened.

"Here's where things get interesting. Rosie didn't identity his remains—the body was identified through personal effects. The head was no longer attached to the body. Long story short, the guy faked his death."

"Are you sure?"

"Totally. Completely. Undoubtedly sure."

Katharine's skin took on a greenish hue.

"Then, in death, he poisoned his wife. And he hunted me down and tried to kill me because I'd found him out. When he was unsuccessful with me, he killed Jon as a way of keeping me away, warning me to mind my own beeswax and shut my mouth."

Katharine shuddered. "This is like an episode of Dateline…"

"On steroids." I finished her sentence. "There's plenty more in the details, but those are a few of the high spots. If you'd like to go home now, I understand."

"Are you kidding me? This is just getting interesting. No wonder you're a wreck. Hell, I'll buy you a carton of cigarettes. If I were you, I'd be smoking *something*."

I released a deep breath I didn't know I'd been holding.

"I don't want you to feel like you have to come with me when I see Judy. This could be dangerous. I can't imagine how or why, because her dad is dead. I'm certain of that, but I don't have any luck at all when these people are involved, so feel free to run another eight miles, or lounge by the pool and sip frozen drinks."

"No way am I missing a minute of this. Paul

doesn't write fiction, but he might want to start when I share this with him."

"You can't. If Jim had even the slightest notion I was here to see Judy, he'd string me up by my earlobes."

"Oh." She zipped a finger across her lips. "Your secret is safe with me."

"Daylight hours seem safest. Shall I suggest tea tomorrow?"

Katharine stood and shook her hands, as if trying to rid herself of pent up anxiety. "I'm up for anything."

"Go take a shower. I'll give her a call back and set something up. Then, I'll shower and we'll go shopping. When I'm this fired up, I need retail therapy."

"That sounds perfect." She trotted out of the room.

I phoned Judy and we agreed that Katharine and I would stop by her house tomorrow at 3 P.M. Her boys wouldn't be home and we'd have time to speak freely.

CHAPTER TWENTY-EIGHT

K YLE'S TIMING COULDN'T have been better. He witnessed Samantha Stitsill leave his sister Judy's house as soon as he pulled in front, but before stepping out of the car. He ducked down in his seat, pretending to search for a lost item on the floor in front of the passenger seat, certain neither she nor her companion, a tall athletic-looking woman, noticed him. He sneered confidently. He was so damned good at deception.

He waited an appropriate time after they left, twelve minutes, before stepping out of his car and knocking on his sister's door.

"Kyle, why I thought…"

"I was someone else." He'd never tell her he'd seen Samantha. Judy could be a turncoat for all he knew. In fact, he decided not to show her what he'd found at Samantha's home. Not yet. Not until he knew whose side she was on.

"I'm so glad you came." She pulled him inside as she glanced over his shoulder. "You brought your things, didn't you? I hope you're staying a while."

He gripped her in a hug. The essence of Samantha filled his senses, just as he'd hoped. She pulled away and held him at arms' length. "Let me look at you. My, you've been spending time at the gym."

"What can I say? I like being in shape for the job."

"Why don't you grab your bags, then tell me all about this new position of yours."

Kyle would never tell her how he'd followed in Dad's footsteps, or fill her in on how much smarter he was than Dad. He'd never sell his soul to the government like Dad, he'd maintain his independence, and only take jobs well-suited to his nature.

What set him apart from his father? Kyle had scruples. Dad would sell his soul to the highest bidder, while Kyle, well, he let his conscience be his guide. He only killed bad people.

CHAPTER TWENTY-NINE

THE EIGHT-MILE run went by in a flicker, Katharine and I were so charged about our meeting with Judy. She'd called and suggested we meet at a local teahouse, since unexpected company had arrived. I readily agreed. A public meeting was far safer than one in the privacy of her home where she could slice us to smithereens and tucked our body parts in her freezer for a year or two before McGrath or any other master investigator discovered our remains.

Plus, the location allowed us time for more retail therapy prior to our meeting and when we passed a wine bar a tad after the noon hour, we fortified ourselves with some resveratrol, to make our hearts stronger—at least I that's how I explained the logic of a midday beverage to Katharine. In reality, I required a steadying drink before our meeting.

I was anxious to know if Judy's proffered friendship was motivated by vengeance. Knowledge of my involvement with her father's death could certainly provoke a desire for retribution. A dicey development, if the case.

I toasted Katharine and sipped my wine before sharing my plan. "Here's what I'm thinking. If you notice Judy about to open up to me, excuse yourself. Pull out your phone and pretend Paul is calling, and you have to take his call, because he's busy later. Step outside and leave us alone for as long as you can without being obvious."

"Roger."

I broke out in laughter and she joined me.

Her eyes sparkled through hysterical tears. "Wait, am I Thelma, or Louise?"

"I don't care," I said, "but whatever you do, don't glance my way while you're keeping yourself occupied outside. If I see your face, I'm going to think of you saying, 'Roger'and fall apart."

"Got it. And since I'm a psychologist, I'll be able to sense her readiness to vomit her life story. There have been times in my career I've wanted to bolt when the situation arises, like when a student begins to share the horror of their abuse, or some similarly tragic story, but I can't imagine wanting to race off when Judy's ready to divulge her innermost secrets."

I bit my lip and peered at her. "You're not going to be a problem, are you?"

"Not at all. I'm yanking your chain is all. Do they have 911 in Canada? If something goes awry, I can be your scout and alert the authorities."

"Funny. I checked before we came. Yes, 911 is the emergency number."

"You devil, you."

I shrugged. "A holdover from my days as a Girl Scout. Always prepared."

We locked eyes, a tad nervous. Me, more than Katharine. For her, this was an adventure. For me, a stark reminder of the sanctity of life. *What the hell was I doing?*

"We may need another drink after our meeting."

"Um, yeah. I'm planning on at least one." Katharine finished her wine in one gulp.

"Ready?"

She stood and smoothed her skirt. "Why yes, Thelma, I am."

We walked the three short blocks to the teahouse, Camellia Sinensis, on St. Joseph Street in the center of Quartier St-Roch. The stenciled teapot on the plate glass window let us know we'd arrived, and Katharine gripped my arm. I took her grasp as a vote of confidence rather than a last ditch effort to tell me she'd changed her mind.

No turning back now.

The shop was divided into two rooms, one an Asian fusion theme café with modern tables and chairs, and the other a classic teashop, where they sold loose tea and other accouterments appropriate for either the novice or avid tea drinker. I'd never seen such a vast assortment of teapots and cups in one place.

In the café, we grabbed a table near the front plate glass window, so Katharine would have a decent view if and when she stepped outside for her phone call. Our plan to arrive early had worked. No sign of Judy yet.

A server approached our table after we settled into our seats.

"Bonjour, madams. Que puis-je faire pour vous?"

Katharine registered the panicked look on my face and spoke for both of us.

"Nous aimerions un peu the."

"Un mélange particulier?"

"Gunpowder organic."

My eyes about popped out of my head, but our server just bowed slightly and vanished.

"It's a fruity flavor…" Katharine shared, "…one I think you'll enjoy."

"Oh my goodness." Those were the last words out of my mouth before I heard my name.

"Samantha? Katharine?"

I spun in my seat to see Judy smiling down at us. I stood and she gathered me in a hug, as if I were a long-lost friend.

Katharine stood, hugged Judy, and offered her the seat closest to the window, across from me. "Sit here. You two have the most to share, and I may need to take a call."

Judy squeezed in front of Katharine and hung her

purse over the back of her chair before lowering herself into it. "Thank you so much for meeting me. Wouldn't you know, a relative showed up unannounced. I'd invited him to visit, but not until the weekend. He caught me off guard."

"No worries. This is lovely and gives us the chance to see more of the city. Katharine speaks French, too, so when I'm in a frenzy over the language, she rescues me."

Judy glanced over at Katharine. "Je suis marquer."

"Merci," Katharine answered.

"I'm officially feeling left out."

They arched their brows at each other.

"No conspiring now," I warned.

The server delivered our tea and three fancy cups.

"I ordered a fruity blend," Katharine offered. "I hope you're a fan."

"Perfect," Judy said.

While Katharine made small talk with Judy, I studied the impostor's daughter. She had gone to a great deal of effort to match her outfit, a stylish skirt with a camisole and featherweight sweater, and had a scarf draped stylishly around her neck. Whenever I wrapped a scarf around my neck, I looked if I'd tied a noose too tight and my face reddened from lack of oxygen.

Her make-up was flawlessly applied and, unlike

the ponytail she wore two days ago when she was ready for the gym, her thick gold tresses were curled and flowed elegantly about her shoulders.

Her sophistication brought her dad to mind. I'd seen him dressed in elegant suits on his best days, but, like a thief in the night, he'd donned a black leather jacket, jeans, a snug beret, and dark gloves on other occasions. In any case, the man oozed grace and style, subtle but unmistakable. Her attire was a stark reminder of her dad, and the similarity unnerved me. Pulling myself together, I continued my assessment. Judy's smile seemed a bit strained, her fingers a bit shaky as she toyed with the handle of her cup.

As tempted as I was to bail her out with small talk, a holdover from my enabling days, I waited her out. Her chatter with Katharine died soon enough, and her silence indicated she had things on her mind.

Katharine jumped from her chair and pulled her phone from her pocket. "Will you look at that? Just as I expected, it's Paul. I hope you understand if I take this call."

Judy and I both nodded, and I waved her away. I watched as she strolled outside, tracking her spot beneath a lamppost, in plain view of our seats. I breathed a sigh of relief. She'd chosen the perfect outlook post.

I focused my attention back on Judy.

"I'm glad your friend had to take the call. I've felt so guilty the past two days. I don't know what compelled me to lie to you, but I told you I hadn't heard from my dad since his time in Botswana, and well, that's just not true. I attended his wedding in Mexico City, to a woman named Beatriz. I don't recall her maiden name, but I know my father had a child with her. Is it wrong I haven't been in touch with them in years?"

"No, of course not. I can't and won't judge your situation. When more than one family is involved, life gets messy. Everyone makes their own choices in these matters."

"My dad was, as I indicated the other day, absent from my life. A lot. When I phoned your home and spoke to your husband, I was hoping I could locate him."

This made no sense. If she had attended her dad's wedding, she must have known he'd settled near us—that's why she called. Or, did I have the facts wrong? I wished I'd kept a log of all of the phone calls and events of those years. All the mysterious clues would come in handy right about now.

"Do you remember when you called? The year? I'm trying to place it in my memory."

"Maybe fifteen years ago. Maybe less. Ten? Eleven? Time passes so quickly. Wait. Let me think. I'd just learned I was pregnant with my oldest boy. So, ten, maybe eleven years ago, depending on the month. I was newly pregnant…that's why I wanted to reach him, to share my news…probably would have been January of 2004."

If memory served me correctly, Stitsill would have been dead then, the first time, from the suicide, unless he'd chosen to fake his death more than once. So, Judy suspected her dad was still alive, and he'd simply moved a few towns away.

No. She *knew* he was alive. She had been the informant on the death certificate and had reported her address as local. I did the math—she'd waited six months after Stitsill faked his death, and then began to look for him. Whether she had spoken to him during that time or not remained to be seen, but either way, she had some understanding of the man her father was.

I wished I could peek inside her soul and read her mind. I'd love to know what she thought of her dad, whether she knew he'd killed my Jon, forced me to question his faithfulness, tried to kill me, and killed my innocent dog. A slow burn consumed me from the tips of my toes to the top of my head. A hot burn, like the blue flame of a fire.

CHAPTER THIRTY

M Y BRAIN WRESTLED with sticky webs of timelines and facts. I refused to give Judy this kind of control. If McGrath were here, in all his investigative glory, he would keep Judy on the hook. Ask her a series of questions and vault the information is his memory.

If I were to accomplish anything from this meeting, I had to glean the truth from the fairy tale.

"When did you last see your father?"

She sank back in her chair and covered her face with her hand. "After his death…" Judy was either consumed with grief, or possessed the acting skills of Sarah Bernhardt. I assumed the latter. I never fell apart any longer when I heard Jon's name, and his death was only two years ago. The memories and the grief were confined to private moments, not a public display. Here Judy was, a puddle of emotion, and her dad had died a decade ago.

The date came to me like a jolt of electricity. June 7, 2004. Judy contacted us before Stitsill's staged

suicide, not after. Either she had lost touch with him as she indicated in her call to Jon, or, she knew where her dad was and somehow figured out he had stolen my husband's identity. Had she tried to interfere with his work? Tried to convince him to change his ways? Probably not. I would have taken that tack, not her. Not everyone has the values I do.

If she saw him after his death, it would have been to identify his remains. McGrath had assured me the guy had been identified by his personal effects. Since he had blown off his head and no family members had viewed the body postmortem, I knew she was lying.

"Were you ever able to reach your dad after you spoke to my husband? What I mean is, did you locate him? I saw photos of you at his wedding to Rosita. Unless you have a twin, you were pictured with your dad in one of the shots she showed me. Your dad's son, Jamie, was a student of mine when he was ten. And as his teacher, his mother shared with me that her husband died in June of 2004. So, you would have talked to him before he died." Close enough, I figured. I'd tutored the young man when Rosie was ill, not taught him in the traditional sense.

She looked like one of my students, caught in a homework lie.

My hopes to back her into an airtight corner by spouting the facts was working. If she were as confused as I was by dates and recreating the past, maybe she'd slip up and say something without having the time to craft her answer.

As I'd guessed, her crying stopped as I asked her questions. "I did attend his wedding, but lost track of him after he and his wife moved to Michigan. If you knew Jamie, then you must also know the other boy, Emilio. Do you know where they are now?"

"No," I lied.

We assumed our positions, just like the boxers in the ring I'd imagined. She wasn't going to give up information without a fight, or at least not without a trade.

"I hope you don't feel like I'm grilling you, but I'm trying to put this together for my own peace of mind. My husband and I were so confused. We received several calls like yours, folks looking for your dad."

"As you said, they were in Michigan, near you. I did speak with my dad once after I talked with your husband, but didn't have the chance to see him before he died."

"I'm sorry."

"You know more about my dad than I do."

"I doubt that."

"You know he was a bad guy."

"I do."

Judy leaned forward, her eyes narrowing to slits. "So let's stop jockeying for position and be straight with each other. What is it you'd like to know?"

I stared at her. "I'm curious what he did for the year after my husband died. I tracked him through some work he did for the State Department. Were you aware of his true profession?"

"I was."

"So you understand he stole my husband's identity."

"I came to the conclusion some time ago, yes. Much more than that I don't know. He changed his name again after his first 'death.'I'm afraid we were both victims of my father's deception."

I wanted to argue—I'd place my losses far above hers—but the room's air slipped away from me, as if I were a balloon with a slow leak. I'd discovered nothing from my conversation with her.

We sat silent for several long moments, each lost in our thoughts.

"Thank you," I finally said.

"For what?"

"For seeing me. I had this ridiculous notion—if I met you, the loose ends I've been attempting to untangle would be tied up, and I'd leave you content in the knowledge that I'd done all I could to bring some closure to this chapter of my life. What I'm realizing is closure is for stories, not real life."

Katharine stood next to me and rested a hand on my shoulder. "Sorry I was gone so long. Paul had some business to discuss with me. How are you ladies doing?"

"I think we've wrapped up our conversation."

Judy stood. "I can't tell you how much I've enjoyed meeting you. If you ever feel like talking, please give me a call on my cell."

I averted my eyes and studied a knot of grain on the table. "Will do."

"And please," she added, "accept my sympathy for the death of your husband, as I accept yours for the death of my father."

CHAPTER THIRTY-ONE

KYLE CHASED JUDY down the street. "You didn't tell her we know, did you?"

"You followed me?"

"Surveillance is part of my daily routine," he admitted. "Hard to turn off the instinct."

A hunter, just like Dad. "Kyle, I'm exhausted, and there is no reason to bother the woman. Dad killed her husband. Let's not dredge up any more skeletons than necessary. Get on with your life, for goodness sake. I'm long past ready to stop glancing over my shoulder. Let's say justice has been served and close the door on Dad. Once and forever."

"Easy for you to say. He's my only relative. You have a mom and sisters, a husband and sons. Who do I have?"

"You have me. And the kids. Brad has turned blue trying to take you under his wing. Why don't you work for him? He's offered you a job on so many occasions and your talents would better be used…in a different creative endeavor, rather than following in

Dad's footsteps."

"What I do isn't a job, but a vocation."

Judy's head throbbed until she feared it would explode. Why she was asking Kyle to stick around was beyond her. The further away he was, the better. She was afraid the evil might ooze from his pores to her kids…infecting them.

But now, she had to worry about him harming Samantha, a perfectly nice person, and a widow. Having another death on her conscience was more than she could bear.

CHAPTER THIRTY-TWO

❝BIG DEAL, YOUR plan didn't work out. Not the end of the world. We still have a few nights left, and it's beautiful. Now, sip your wine and settle down.❞

"You're absolutely right. There were no guarantees, and I did confirm my suspicions. Stitsill was a gangster. And while I shouldn't be surprised the U.S. government has guys like him on the payroll, I'm disturbed just the same." I fought like hell to keep my knees from knocking, but I'd lost all control. Judy's final words haunted me. I cautioned myself. *You're imaging things. She didn't have a hidden agenda. It's over.*

"And you should be. Certainly, you can't go to a politician and cry foul. You'd just wind up putting your family in jeopardy again. Not only that, but you have a perfectly good man waiting for you in Maine. He's recovering his memory, which means your life is falling into place for once. You've endured mountains of heartache, and happiness and contentment are foreign to you at this point, but as your friend, I encourage you to grab on by your fingers and toes and enjoy the ride."

"You have a valid point," I said. "I've spent the past few years in crisis mode of one sort or another. I'm not sure I even know how to live a normal life any longer. I'm always waiting for another branch to fall on my head."

"You need time to adjust. Let's do something fun. What's your pleasure?"

"How about we drive back to the hotel? We are staying in this amazing city and other than running along the river and shopping, we haven't seen the sights. Do you like history? We could visit the fort. I imagine the view from the walls is spectacular. Let's rent bikes."

"Perfect."

We linked arms and strolled along the street to the car.

"I've been so wrapped up in my own life, I didn't ask. Did you talk with Paul?"

"Yes, but we can save the conversation about him for another time."

"Absolutely not. Tell me."

"He's going through the usual jealousy. He does much better when I'm home each night to tuck him in."

"I'm worried about you. You try so hard to be upbeat and pretend you're happy about deciding to stay with Paul, but do you ever think how life might have gone had you decided on Ben?"

"I've never had the opportunity to entertain the option."

"Take time now."

"It hurts too much."

"Humor me. Unless you're absolutely sure you don't want to go there."

"No, trust me, I fight going there all the time, when I hear a song on the radio, pass someone wearing Ben's cologne—the tiniest thing provokes a downward spiral. On the occasions I run into him, I'm immediately transported back. Not to a memory necessarily…it's as if a spirit consumes me and my arms prickle with desire. It sounds hokey, but it's true."

"Tell me more. I think I've had the same thing happen."

"I'm transported to another world. Back to the days when we were a sinners'couple. We were easy together. Even at the time, I was aware of how special we were. Touching his hand was magic. Brushing the hair on his arms, the warmth of his lips on mine. More though, we had this unspoken understanding of how deeply we loved each other. We didn't need reassurances. We just knew." A faraway look enveloped her face.

A chill passed through me. I recalled a similar feeling when I met Jon, and when I first laid eyes on

McGrath. "I wish we could bottle the elixir."

Katharine locked eyes with me. "This wave of vicious emptiness crashes over me on the heels of the best memories. Remembering hurts."

"Because you love another man."

"Don't get me wrong. I love Paul. He's a great guy, and I couldn't ask for a more devoted husband. But he's so dependent on me, I struggle for oxygen sometimes."

"Just because Paul's a great guy doesn't mean you should sacrifice your happiness. You have lots of good years ahead of you."

"Can we not talk about this anymore?"

"The guilt?"

"Yes, and this pain in my chest."

"Race you to the car," I said, as I took off.

Katharine passed me within seconds.

***

I stopped the doorman and asked, "Can you tell us where a bike rental is? We'd like to ride through Old Quebec."

"There's one just past the gate at Porte St. Louis. On the left."

Katharine gripped my arm. "I know the exact location. I ran past the place the other day."

We changed into shorts and T-shirts, stuffed money, cell phones, and room keys in our pockets, and rode the elevator downstairs. Fifteen minutes later, we had two bikes, stylish helmets with neon pink racing stripes running over the top, well suited for our Thelma and Louise duo, bike locks, maps, and bottled water.

The weather was sublime. Not too hot, maybe seventy-five degrees, with bright sunshine and a cooling breeze drifting off the river.

"Want me to go first?" I had checked the map and the route seemed easy enough to follow. There was only one big downhill, which would mean walking our bikes up on the return trip, but I reasoned we'd be ready to work a different set of muscles by then.

"Lead on, pathfinder."

I hopped on the bike after adjusting the helmet one last time, and tucking my water bottle into its holder. The scenery was spectacular. I'd grown up a city girl, but not like this, in the midst of the hustle and bustle. There were as many pedestrians as bicyclists, the sidewalks were narrow, and cars whizzed past us on the street. We took a right on Rue du Fort, another on Cote de la Montagne, which means "Hill of the Mountain" and viewed the knoll stretched out before us. I had visions of the long lost bravery of my youth, back when I'd lift my feet from the pedals and my grip from the handlebars and fly downhill like a freefalling stone. Today, I white-knuckled the handgrips and tried to anticipate the sharp curves I'd witnessed on the map, determined to do my best not to kill any pedestrians or crash into any motorists.

The streets were lined with shops, residences above the storefronts, all made of brick and stone—a trip into another century.

"We've ridden into the past," Katharine shouted from behind me. I slowed down and she pulled up right next to me.

"This was the absolute best idea. My head is clearer, and my heart lighter."

"And we can reward ourselves with a glass of wine when we finish."

Katharine darted ahead of me to avoid a child who'd darted into our path. I swerved to the right. Thankfully, we left him as we found him, and soon met the river's edge. As if the world opened up to us, a bike path stretched along the near bank and we enjoyed a smooth ride for the next couple of kilometers.

The city to our right, the river to our left, reminded me of a similar setting in Chicago, tankers and ferryboats dotting the water, the bustle of city life in the background.

There were few cars along this stretch. My blood pressure dropped. I let go, envisioning a life with my recovered detective—a cozy little family, my five kids and him. We could erect a white picket fence, and instead of becoming a private eye, I saw myself as a dedicated teacher, mother and wife, focusing on the little things, like lingering over a glass of Cabernet with my new husband, watching the kids grow up and leave us behind in our cozy little nest.

The sudden urge to call McGrath and say, "Let's plan our wedding,"—to not wait a moment longer to begin living—gripped me like the tentacles of an octopus. I almost pulled out my phone and dialed, but I knew what I klutz I could be when walking, let alone riding.

As soon as we made it back to the hotel, while Katharine showered, I'd call him. I couldn't wait.

CHAPTER THIRTY-THREE

THE SCREECHING OF brakes was the first sound I heard, before being slammed from behind, hearing the crunch of metal and the blaring of horns. I remember flying through the air, helpless, like a rag doll, my first thoughts of Katharine. Had she been hit, too?

What happened next, I don't recall. I have no idea how much time passed, what day it was, where I was. After a while, I heard sirens off in the distance, and in the recesses of my mind, I wanted to scream as I was jostled by men with deep voices.

By the time I came to, or became lucid enough to take in my surroundings, I recognized hospital walls and the rails of a hospital bed. A minute or two later the room to come into better focus, and I stared at the fluorescent light over my head. My head pounded when I tried to move—my right arm was encased in a cast, as well as my right ankle.

I inched my head to my right, no roommate. No bed even. For some reason, they'd placed me in a single room. Katharine was nowhere to be seen. My heart skipped a beat and my breathing became shallow.

A call button hung over the side rail of the bed, but on my right side, my bad side. I couldn't reach the damn thing with my left, not unless I rolled onto my broken arm. After what seemed like an eternity, I was able to touch my fingertips to the button, inch it between my fingers and push the circle with my index finger.

I blinked in an attempt to keep tears at bay. I had no idea what to say, but desperately needed to know Katharine was okay.

A French speaking voice came over the speaker. "Comment puis-je vous aider?"

Closing my eyes, I rifled my memory banks. "Vous" meant "you." "Aider," aid or help. But I couldn't recall enough French to speak. After a long moment, I said, "Aider, merci." Then I remembered, "merci" meant "thank you." I substituted, "se il vous plaît?"

Five eternal minutes later, a nurse entered my room, wearing a scowl that would haunt a Marine.

"Excusé moi. Parle un pue le Francais."

Her beady eyes bore into me. I wasn't in Kansas any more. Just then, another woman entered. She took a swift glance at the nurse and hurried to my bedside. "I can help you." She spun around and said to the nurse, "Je vais l'aider." She would help me.

The nurse flipped on her heel and swept out of the room.

"What can I help you with?"

"My friend," I said. "She was with me when I was hit. I don't know if she was involved in the accident, but her name is Katharine Nelson. Could you please check for me? I'm so worried."

"I just came on duty an hour ago. I think you've been here since yesterday afternoon. Let me see what I can find out. In the meantime, can I get you anything? Something to eat? Drink? I'd offer you a menu, but it's written only in French. As you can see, there is some resistance among some of the staff to speak English."

"Soup, perhaps? Crackers? Some water?"

"I'll bring your food first. You must be starving. Then, I'll see about your friend." She patted my hand and offered me a sympathetic gaze.

Tears welled in my eyes. If I could only click my heels together and be home. In Lexington. With my kids. And McGrath.

Where the hell is my phone? If I could reach McGrath, everything would be okay. I watched the clock. Katharine and I had headed off on our bikes around 4:30 P.M. I'd been here almost twenty-four hours if what the nurse's aide said was true. My heart pounded in my chest. *Where was Katharine*?

The aide returned with a tray and set it on the side table and swung the entire contraption in front of me. I dabbed at my tears with the napkin and thanked her.

"I'll go see about your friend. Sit tight. Try not to worry."

Easier said than done. "Oh, wait. Do you know what happened to my personal belongings? I need to make a call. It's important."

She strode to the small nightstand beside my bed and pulled open the bottom drawer, then yanked a plastic bag from inside, placed the bag on the bed, and opened the sack for me. "Would you like me to look?"

"Si vous plait," I said.

I peered at her name tag as she bent over the side of the bed. Michelle.

"Here," she said. "Shall I dial for you?"

Overcome with tears, I didn't think I could speak to McGrath, and now that I had my phone, I didn't know what to say. I couldn't yet report on Katharine's condition. I had no idea where she was, but in my heart I knew she would have been at my side if she was able to move. We hadn't known each other long, but the bond was as strong as cement.

"Please, if you can find out about my friend first, I'll call when I have news to report."

"You could call and tell your loved ones where you are, and then when I come back, phone again."

I studied the battery life on my phone. Eleven percent. Too risky.

"No, I'd better wait. Thank you though."

Michelle squeezed my shoulder before leaving the room. I hate to even think what she would discover, so I simply laid there, unable to do anything more than pray.

CHAPTER THIRTY-FOUR

MICHELLE FOUND KATHARINE in intensive care, still unconscious, a Jane Doe—one of two Jane Does to be exact. From what Michelle read on her chart, Katharine had a broken patella, tibia and fibula in her right leg. She had undergone surgery to pin and wire her patella back together. The reason for her comatose state wasn't addressed on her chart, so Michelle called in a nurse.

"Can you tell me about Jane Doe in Room 1772?"

"Why, do you know her?"

"Maybe. Was she brought in as the result of a car/bike collision?"

The intensive care nurse, Carrie, replied with a nod.

"Her friend is on the fifth floor."

"Write down her name for me, please. Nice to know who we've got here."

"Is she going to be all right? Mrs. Stitsill is anxious to know about her friend."

"Yes. She's still disoriented from the pain meds and her recent surgery, but other than limping around for a good long while, she should make a full recovery. Admitting is anxious to gather the insurance information on her. Do you know where the ladies are from? No one's come looking for them and more than a day's gone by."

"The States is all I know. My poor patient doesn't speak French and Sarge downstairs was about ready to toss her out the window."

"The older gals are like that sometimes. Tradition and all."

Michelle agreed and hurried to the stairs. Her patient's anxiety level would drop significantly once she learned her friend had survived the accident.

***

She entered the room with a huge smile painted on her face. "Good news. I found your friend."

A wave of relief washed over me. "Thank God."

"She's pretty banged up. Her kneecap is broken and both bones in her lower leg. Last night, because the wound was exposed, she had surgery to repair the patella."

"Did you tell her I'm here and doing well?"

"She's not awake now, but that's due to her recent surgery and the medication. I told her nurse all about you, so she will let Katharine know when she wakes up."

"I can't thank you enough. What room is she in? I want to give her family a call and let them know. Any idea how long we will be here?"

"I'm guessing a few days. But even when you're discharged, you'll both have some recovery ahead of you."

"I understand. We're staying at the Fairmont. As I'm sure you gathered, we're from the States."

"Tell me your full name," Michelle said. "The hospital will want to get your insurance and contact information as soon as they can."

"Samantha Stitsill. My insurance information is at the hotel, and," she hesitated, "we don't really know anyone in the city."

"Do you think a relative will join you? Neither of you will be able to drive, considering your injuries."

"I'm about to make a call."

"I'll leave you alone then."

"Thank you so much for your help."

"It's my pleasure," she said as she opened the door. "And when you need something, just ask for me when you buzz the nurse's station. I'll do whatever I can."

I closed my eyes for a brief moment. Life lessons were being delivered to me on a daily basis. I'd better heed them.

McGrath's cell rang twice before he picked up. "Sam, are you okay? I was trying to give you space, but not hearing from you in over twenty-four hours has me in a bit of a panic."

"I'm fine, but there's been an accident."

McGrath's breathing became ragged. "Where are you?"

"I'm in a hospital in Quebec. Katharine and I went on a bike ride down by the river and before I knew what happened, I woke up here. I'm not sure who or what hit me, but I remember the sound of brakes screeching, so I'm guessing I was hit by a car, then either slid into Katharine so she fell too, or the car careened into her after hitting me."

"Thank God you're okay. I'm heading to the car right now. Ben and I are at the Jack Russell having a drink, but if I start driving now, I can be there by morning."

"No, don't rush off. Get a good night's sleep. My phone battery is running low, so call the hospital and ask for my room."

I gave him the information, then remembered wanting to call him yesterday. Part of me wanted to wait until he arrived to tell him, part of me felt an urgency to tell him right away.

"Jim?"

"Yes?"

"I don't want to wait to get married. Let's make plans as soon as we can."

I heard the smile behind his words. "Life's too short," he said, then ended the call.

***

Despite my better judgment, I pressed the nurse's call button. To my surprise, Michelle answered my call. "What can I do for you, Samantha?"

"When you have a chance, could you stop in for a minute? No rush."

She arrived twenty minutes later.

"Would it be possible for you to arrange a wheelchair for me and have someone take me up to see Katharine? I'd feel so much better if I saw her with my own eyes."

"How about we visit her in the morning? I'll check with her nurse tonight, and leave word for her to notify you if anything changes. As it is now, Katharine's sleeping, and both of you need rest."

With trepidation, I agreed.

"I'm on duty until eleven. I promise I'll check with her nurse when my shift ends, then let you know how she's doing before I leave. Deal?"

"Deal."

CHAPTER THIRTY-FIVE

A HAND WARMED mine as I awoke, and I opened my eyes to see my favorite guy sitting bedside. We'd spent more time in hospitals than I cared to recall, but in his calming presence I swore I could climb a mountain, swim the Atlantic, or maybe, make my way to the bathroom with help.

"You're here."

"Yes, ma'am. A little worse for the drive, but I figure I can shower at your hotel and make myself presentable. You don't mind if Ben comes along, do you?"

A lump caught in my throat. "Wait, did you say, Ben? You mean Paul, don't you?"

"No, I mean Ben. He insisted I not drive alone, and we went by the Nelson's but Paul was AWOL, so I left a note. We buzzed by Ben's house for his passport after stopping at Paul and Katharine's, and were on our way. We shared the driving and some fast food."

I searched the room. "Where is he?"

"Upstairs. With Katharine."

If possible, my head sank deeper into my pillow.

Letting go of events outside of my control has always been an issue for me, and rather than lie there in abject shock and terror, I was dying to rush upstairs and talk to my friend. Warn her before she awoke, allow her time to process Ben's arrival, sort out whether she even wanted to see him.

The past two days had altered my world and caused me to make some life-changing decisions. How Katharine would process our accident might mean she'd do the same. I wanted to caution her against making any rash decisions. Not like my decision to marry McGrath was impulsive, but I had to admit my brush with the harsh reality of beating the odds spurred me to speed up the process.

Considering how much angst a simple conversation about Ben had caused Katharine earlier, seeing him when she awakened might cause cardiac arrest, or worse, she might think she'd died. Then again, once she saw his face, she might think she'd gone to heaven.

I wondered what he'd say to her. How he felt about her. In another life, I might be a matchmaker.

"Did Ben talk about Katharine on your drive? Spending five and a half hours in the car with someone provides the opportunity for serious conversation. Or did you talk sports and carving the entire time?"

McGrath puffed out his chest. "You'll be proud to know I pierced his armor. He and Katharine had an affair over six years ago. His wife and baby were killed shortly after in a horrific car accident, but by then, Katharine had married Paul. Then, two years after they married, Paul had his accident."

McGrath's gaze fell to the floor. He closed his eyes and took a steadying breath. "So much tragedy makes me thankful. We still have an intact family."

My eyes widened. Had he forgotten my husband was killed?

He noticed my shocked expression. "I'm not trying to be a clod, but we have each other. Ben has no one. He lost his wife, his daughter, and Katharine. He's gone on with his life in spite of losing his family, but...Katharine is still alive. I can assure you, he's still wrestling with his love for her. He's determined he can't, or won't, do anything to hurt her marriage."

"She told me the story, and she's still in love with him too. But she's torn."

"You always say everything happens for a reason. This was meant to be."

I squeezed my eyes shut tight. "But Paul has to be notified. I wonder if the hospital reached him yet."

"Someone would have had to pass along his phone number. You didn't. I'm guessing Katharine hasn't been able to call him. From what the nurse said, she was pretty groggy when we arrived and hadn't been too lucid since the accident and her surgery. It's entirely possible he doesn't know about the accident yet."

"Should we get in touch with him?"

"Not our place."

"Now, you're being a matchmaker. If I'd been hurt and Katharine didn't let you know, you'd be furious."

He winked. "Give them a little time together. The man drove six hours with me, and he's tired and hungry. He should have some small reward for his efforts."

I scowled, unsure how to handle advising Paul, and bit the inside of my cheek. Why I think I'm in charge of structuring the universe, I have no clue.

"Let this go, Sam. Not your concern."

"Paul will be livid."

"I'm not sure he needs to know. Leave fate alone, would you?"

"Fate."

He stroked my hand. "Fate brought us together. The first night I saw you, you changed me. Like a bugle reveille, you woke my sleeping heart, and I couldn't rest until I saw you again. Being around you makes me feel complete, connected. If I never saw another person as long as I lived, I'd be the happiest man in the world. Just think what might have happened if you hadn't been at the Frozen Margarita to hear your brother's band—or I'd gone directly home from work rather than stop for a beer. And then

I was the cop who took Rosie's call, which led me back to you. Tell me that wasn't fate."

"You're right. We couldn't have orchestrated any of those scenarios if we were Houdini. I never wanted Jon to die. And I feel guilty now, because I was attracted to you when he was still alive, but I'm learning to let myself off the hook. Give me some credit. I said 'yes.'"

His eyes twinkled when he smiled and his dimples deepened. "You're just displaying good judgment."

"I need to kiss you."

He offered me a stubbled cheek, and I lifted my hand to bring him closer, so I could breathe in his scent and stroke the back of his head. This man was a gift I wasn't sure I deserved.

He kissed me with such tenderness I wanted to melt. I rested my head against his cheek and my entire body relaxed. Even my broken arm stopped screaming at me. The swelling in my ankle subsided, or so it seemed.

After a long moment, McGrath sat back and brushed the hair off my face.

"I consider myself the luckiest man in the world. In spite of the steady crises, we are so lucky."

I locked eyes with him and held his gaze.

We were.

***

At my insistence, McGrath trod off to check on Ben and Katharine. I suggested he and Ben go to the hotel and grab a shower, catch a bit of shuteye, and let the patients rest for a while.

Michelle, my favorite nurse's aide, wasn't due to arrive for several hours, but if I planned this right, she'd be on duty while the guys were gone, and I could slip up to Katharine's room, or at least phone her room and talk to her. Letting Paul know about the accident was the right thing to do, and even if he didn't want to head to Quebec, he needed to be aware of her injuries. Considering his inability to walk, caring for Katharine might prove dicey.

While lost in thought, I missed the opening of my room door until a man cleared his throat and caught my attention. A tall, sturdy French policeman, in a dark navy uniform with gold stripes up the outside seams of his trousers and a snugly knotted necktie, surprised me.

He said, "Bonjour," which I managed to answer, but then I was at a loss to communicate with him. He gestured to his note pad and made a scribbling motion with his pen. He had come to take an accident report.

We'd need an interpreter in order for me to give him the few details I remembered. There had to be witnesses, didn't there?

He held up a finger, letting me know he'd return in a moment, and as he left the room, a vision of

Dudley Do-right came to mind. I'd expected the mounted police, not this man. I held my own private chuckling party until he reappeared in the doorway several minutes later, this time with an older volunteer, white tight-curled hair haloing her face, with a set of pale blue eyes to match her coat.

"Hello," she started, and then explained what I already knew. Officer Bernard had come to hear what I remembered of the accident.

I recalled what I could, which took about sixty seconds, then asked, "Were there witnesses?"

I waited while she translated and paused for the officer's answer.

"Yes," she said, "but they weren't able to catch the driver of the car. He sped off before anyone could stop him, and by the time they called the authorities, he was long gone."

"What kind of car? I saw a flash of white before I was hit, and heard a car's brakes screech. Was anyone able to write down the license plate number? Do the police have any leads?"

I glanced back and forth between the two of them, chatting faster than I could blink, and picked up not a word of what they were saying.

"Things happened suddenly and the drivers who stopped were more interested in getting you and your friend the help you needed than pursuing the driver of the vehicle. Witnesses weren't able to give much information other than they thought the driver was

Caucasian and the car was a white Ford Focus."

Officer Barnard spoke to the volunteer, and then she explained. "The officer will also speak to your friend now. Maybe she can help."

"Merci," I said. "I hope so."

They said goodbye and left. Prickles rose on my arms and my headache returned times three.

CHAPTER THIRTY-SIX

I MUST HAVE suffered from post traumatic stress disorder, because I imagined Judy having run me down as revenge for killing her father. Tempering my ongoing paranoia would require years of total monotony, and the likelihood of tedium arriving on my doorstep was nil.

I talked myself down—Judy would never try to hurt me, she was a mom with a family, and moms are good people, but my mistrust was as innate as my hair color. Her gene pool tugged at me. Along with the way she'd parted from the teashop with the words, "Accept my sympathy for the death of your husband, as I accept yours in the death of my father," almost like a warning.

Still, for her to have followed Katharine and me back to the hotel, waited for us to change and stroll to the rental shop, then follow us on our bike ride and mow us down—the scenario seemed too farfetched.

McGrath sauntered through the door, his eyes alight with pride, and his hands behind his back. He pulled out a bouquet of roses and bent over to kiss me.

"Are you taking lessons from Ben?"

"How'd you guess?"

I narrowed my eyes. "He didn't."

"Did."

I grumbled. "That's horrible. Is Katharine awake? She's going to kill me. Does she think I had you bring Ben? How is she? Does she seem upset? Nervous?"

"Stop yammering for a minute, and I'll give you the full report."

I zipped my lips and cocked my head, waiting.

He paused, lingering on his thoughts.

"Would you hurry up? The suspense is killing me. Tell me everything. Where was he when you went in the room? In a chair by the bed? Sitting on the edge of the bed? Cuddled up with her?"

When he shot me a "shut up" eyeball, I zipped my lips again—and "threw away the key" this time.

"His back was facing me when I walked in. He was talking to her, in soft tones, like he always does—the calm, soothing voice of instruction."

"The let-me-show-you-the-way voice."

McGrath crossed his arms and dropped his head.

"Sorry, go ahead," I said.

"I listened hard because I knew you'd want details. He was telling her he'd never stopped loving her."

"Oh my God, that's wonderful. I mean, it's

dreadful. The poor thing. How did she take it?"

"Contrary to your current belief, Katharine is a strong, independent woman. She's not a bumbling idiot. I have faith she can take care of herself."

"How did she respond? What did she say?"

"She said she loved him too, but she had a life already. One too full for him to be included."

Air escaped my lungs as if I'd been sucker-punched, and I struggled to take a breath. Tears welled in my eyes.

"Hey." McGrath set my flowers on the bed stand, sat at my side, and gripped my hand. "You're tired and you've been through a tremendous trauma. Why don't you get some rest? I'll take Ben to the hotel and we'll clean up."

"My key card should be in my shorts pocket."

He rifled through my belongings and came out with the card.

"Be back in an hour or two."

***

I counted to two thousand once McGrath had left the room. Then I pressed the call button. When Michelle answered, I closed my eyes in relief. She answered by saying, "Be there in a few minutes."

She shifted her eyes when I asked her to wheel me to Katharine's room, but when my bottom lip quivered, she relented and asked me to point her toward my hospital issued comb. "We can't have you visiting in such disarray."

Fifteen minutes later, sponged, brushed, and with fresh breath, she found a wheelchair and pushed me up to Katharine's room. Once she wheeled me inside, she told me she'd be back in twenty minutes. "Both you and your friend need your rest."

I thanked her, and patted Katharine's hand. Her eyes were closed, and a peaceful aura shrouded her. Ben had the same effect on everyone he spent time with.

"Hey, you," I encouraged. With a gentle shake of her arm, I tried to rouse her again. "Katharine, I'm here."

Her eyes peeked open and the slightest grin formed on her lips. "Hey. How are you?"

I inched my chair closer with my good foot. "Better than you, I'm guessing."

"I'm great, actually. For once, my dream was real and not imagined. Did you know Ben was coming?"

"No, but when I heard, I worried you'd think I'd put Jim up to bringing him along. You know Jim tried to reach Paul, right?"

"Yes, he told me."

Her face was drawn and the circles beneath her eyes a deep shade of gray. My lungs pinched and I clutched my chest—no doubt another wave of PTSD.

"I can't take the suspense. Tell me what you're thinking."

A soft chuckle erupted from the back of her throat, followed by eyes as wide as silver dollars. "I'm not divorcing my husband tomorrow or anything, but I do have a lot to think about. Seeing Ben brought back memories and feelings I've tamped down for a long, long time."

"Do you have electricity trickling through your blood?"

"Just like junior high. I have to call Paul though. Do you have your cell?"

I lifted my iPhone from my lap. "Right here. And my nurse lent me her charger, so it's ready to go. I have international calling for the entire month, so you can talk as long as you like. Do you think Paul will come?"

"I'm not sure. This is a busy week for him. He has some book signings, but I don't remember when."

I went quiet for a moment and blinked.

"Stop," Katharine said. "I see you concocting a plan."

"I'm not. But I am thinking you'd benefit from a few days with Ben before we head home. I can't imagine either one of us are ready to travel, plus, the police might find out who hit us, and we might have to testify or something. Did you see what happened?"

"Not really. I veered toward the side of the road when I heard brakes squealing and called out for you, but then everything went black and the next thing I heard was sirens and a crowd of murmuring voices. I remember someone telling me I'd be okay, but nothing more until I woke up here."

I scraped my teeth over my lip. "I don't care if they figure out who did this. The sooner we get out of this godforsaken place and back to Maine, the better."

"Agreed. Let's not drive too fast though."

"We have two cars, you know. Maybe you and Ben should drive together, and Jim and me."

Katharine went quiet. "Maybe," she said after a long moment.

A soft knock sounded, and the door opened. A young man stood holding a huge arrangement of flowers. Even though he wore casual clothes, I detected a bit of discomfort in his affect.

"Are you Katharine Nelson?" he asked.

My jaw tightened. "Who are you?"

"Florist delivery, ma'am."

"Set it on the table, please," I said.

He placed the large container on the table, and nodded our way before leaving the room. His gaze held mine for an uncomfortably long minute, as if he knew me, or had seen me somewhere before, then abruptly spun around and hurried out the door.

My suspicions kicked in again. "Odd."

"Stop second-guessing people, Sam."

"Tell me this. Ben brought you flowers." I pointed to the vase on the bed stand. "Who else knows you're in the hospital?"

"Oh," she said, her brow knitting. "Check for a

card."

With only one functional arm and one working leg, I nudged the wheelchair over to the table, fastened the chair's brakes and inched my way to its edge and eased myself up. Tucked inside the hydrangea, I discovered a tiny white envelope.

"Go ahead. Open the damned thing," Katharine said as I hesitated.

I pulled the card out and read aloud, "Best wishes for a full and complete recovery." I flipped over the card. "No signature."

"That's strange."

"Not in my world." I sank back into the chair with a sigh, while my heart sank from my chest to my stomach.

"What do you think is going on? Did you receive one?"

"Not yet. But, I'll bet I find one in my room when I get back."

I tapped my foot. Where was Michelle? She said twenty minutes.

"Calm down," Katharine said.

"I know. You're right. I don't trust anyone."

"If you're thinking Judy is somehow responsible for our accident, I disagree. I'm a psychologist, remember? I size folks up for a living. Her sympathy for Jon's loss was genuine. And, from what you told me about your conversation, reasonable."

"Noted. I'm a nervous wreck. When Jim comes

back, I'll feel better. He and Ben can take care of us as well as anyone at the hospital. Let's see when we can be discharged."

Katharine's eyebrows about hit the ceiling. "I have to call Paul."

"Take my phone. Feel free to answer if anyone calls. Jim can retrieve it once he and Ben come back. Meanwhile, my room number is 1434. Call my extension after you talk to Paul and fill me in."

"Will do," she said.

Michelle strolled into the room. "Ready?" she asked.

"Sure." I glanced back at Katharine as Michelle wheeled me away. "Take care of you. No guilt."

"Yes, ma'am."

CHAPTER THIRTY-SEVEN

I SLEPT FOR a solid hour once Michelle helped me back into bed. When I awoke, I smelled more than just the roses. Flowers' fragrance filled my senses and I tilted my head toward the aroma. On the tray table sat a gorgeous display of pink lilies. A knot of dread filled my stomach. A part of me wanted to put this puzzle together, the other part wanted to hide my face beneath the covers and never come out.

With the bed control just out of reach, I wriggled over to grab the darned thing and press the button, raising the head of the bed so I could stretch my fingers far enough to pluck the card from the bouquet. If I had been standing, my knees surely would have buckled when I read the card.

The message was identical to the one Katharine received. No signature either. More importantly, it wasn't addressed to me—the recipient's name was missing. As if it had purposely been left off. I did a mental playback. When the deliveryman entered Katharine's room, he knew her name. I pressed the call button and Michelle answered.

"Did you see someone deliver flowers to my room? There's no name on the card, and no one knows I'm here. I'm afraid they've been delivered to me by mistake."

"No, they're yours. I directed the delivery to your room when the gentleman brought them up."

"What did he look like?"

"The deliveryman? Nothing special. Probably thirty or so. Average build. Sandy hair. Polo shirt."

Same description as the guy who delivered Katharine's flowers, but Michelle's description could apply to about anyone. "Thanks. I must have a secret admirer. I'll enjoy them."

Goose bumps peppered my arms and my hands tingled. I searched for my phone, to call McGrath and fess up about my visits with Judy Carver, and remembered I had left the damned thing with Katharine. I nearly bit my lip bloody with apprehension.

Once again, I'd succeeded in putting a friend's life in jeopardy, along with my own. All I wanted was to get the hell out of this godforsaken place, as fast as my wheelchair would carry me. And to live a life of uninspired normalcy, in a house that resembled every other house, with a steady husband and strong father for my kids, and maybe even a dog. Suburbia times seven.

The door opened and McGrath sauntered in.

Something about him had changed. I'd missed the transformation in the aftermath of the accident, but I read the clues like the flashing walk sign on a street corner. His eyes were clearer, and the constant tension his jaw had worn since the accident had finally relaxed. Maybe carving had given him a sense of satisfaction.

"What's going on with you?" I asked.

"Hello to you, too," he answered, then planted a long, delicious kiss on my lips.

"Pull up a chair and tell me all about it."

The chair screeched across the floor as he pushed closer to me. He dropped into the recliner and leaned forward, looking quite pleased with himself. "I've remembered. Everything. Most everything, I'd guess. The shooting, the travels to Japan, past cases I've worked on." He beamed, but his eyes were misty.

Tears rimmed my eyes and a lump clogged my throat. "Wow."

"I used to be married to a wretched woman. I spent time as a beat cop before becoming a detective, I went to high school with a guy named Gary Connors and we kicked some serious ass at the State Regionals game my senior year. The first car I owned was a '72 Ford Focus. You made me wait for almost a solid year before you slept with me. Annie hated me when I first met her. The kids teased you about having a boyfriend."

"I can't tell you how happy I am. This is the best

news we've had in a year. I love you, Jim McGrath."

His shoulders widened as he leaned back in the chair. "Now you can marry me, knowing full well what you're signing up for."

"We need to hightail our way out of here and back to Maine. You know my cockamamie notion to quit teaching and become a PI, like Kyra Sedgwick on the Closer, or Marg Helgenberger on C.S.I.? What I really want is a normal life, teaching by day, chasing my kids around by night, snuggling up with you on the weekends. Can we do that?"

"It would be my preference. We're a dynamic team with the kids. How about I share details of cases and you can help me flush them out? I say, let's get back to Maine, I'll finish my gig at the museum and we head to the lake and share the news with the kids. In person."

My face lit up. "Yes. Yes. Yes."

I told him then about meeting with Judy, both at her house and the teashop. I filled him in on the unexpected flower deliveries to both Katharine and me. He rolled his eyes and clenched his jaw, his hand cupping his chin.

"Are you ready to stop this madness?"

"Trust me, I've reformed. This accident, whether somebody ran me down on purpose or not, has jolted my sanity back into place. I'm done sorting out mysteries and digging up skeletons. Let's see when we can get out of here. Maybe Ben and Katharine want a room of their own for a couple of days."

"You're a troublemaker, Sam. I thought you were ready to mind your own business and enjoy mundane tasks. As a matter of fact, I have a few ideas of my own. We can practice your new lease on normal." He pushed back the covers. "How about I climb in bed with you?"

"And bang against these plaster casts? Yeah, I can see that happening. Go find a doctor and see when I can get out of here."

McGrath smoothed his pant legs when he stood and straightened his shoulders. His confidence had returned full tilt, and my heart swelled. I had my man back.

While he was gone, I played with ideas. Maybe we should move away, start fresh. New house. New schools. No. I was acting crazy again. Guess I had no clue about simplicity. My head began to throb.

The phone rang and jerked me out of self-deprecation mode. "Hello?"

"Hi," Katharine said, her voice so soft I could barely hear.

"What happened?"

"Paul isn't coming. I minimized the accident and my injuries. Funny thing is, I didn't plan to, but the words tumbled out of me like well-rehearsed lines."

"You don't want him to come. You want some time with Ben."

"I'm hot from the inside out."

"You aren't sick, it's the shame and the guilt."

Katharine grumbled. "I know, and I hate this. Why can't I go on with my life and lock these feelings away?"

"Life's not so simple."

A long silence ensued. I tried to think of words to soothe her aching heart. I recognized her angst from my own past, realizing how triggers never go away and can so easily be reignited when we least suspect—a song, a scent, the sound of a voice. We carry our history wherever we go, no matter which fork in the road we choose.

But her past was alive, while mine was dead. There was no way to know which was the harder of the two, but part of me felt her future held opportunities in the same way mine did, and I wanted her to be happy.

"Things might work out with Paul. Maybe seeing Ben will be a catalyst for you two, there's no way to know. No crystal ball. But, here's what I think. Let the situation with Ben play out. Enjoy every single moment with him. Revel in his touch, hang on his every word, commit the sound of his voice to your memory. His eyes crinkle when he grins. Hold those smile lines in your heart. He loves you. You love him. Life is short. Too short. Every chance you have to love someone is a gift. Treasure the gift.

"In the end, you'll be glad you did. At the least, you might have some fun. At the most, you might gain some closure. You've held onto each other in spite of years apart, and you both need an answer to the burning question, 'Will we ever be together?'After some time with him, you'll be better able to make a decision.

"Paul is a good guy. I get that. But if you're not happy with him, you both deserve better."

"I might throw up," she said.

"You might."

McGrath poked his head through the doorway.

"Hey, Jim's back. Did Ben just show up, too?"

"Yep, just popped in."

"I'm hoping we can blow this joint. Check with your nurse and have her hound the doctor. As long as we're in Quebec, we might as well enjoy the visit, even if we are confined to the hotel. At least we can sip fruity drinks at the bar."

I handed the phone to McGrath, who cradled the receiver and then folded his arms in front of him. "Here's the dope. You'll be casted for at least four weeks. You might require a bit of physical therapy after the cast is removed, and you'll need crutches for a while." He tipped his head and examined my casts. "Could be tricky with your injuries both on the same side. Good thing is, you have an able-bodied mate right here, and I'm bound and determined to spring you so we can catch up. In any case, they'll try to discharge you tomorrow, if you check out well with the doctors in the morning."

"What about Katharine? Any word on her?"

"I'll go see."

CHAPTER THIRTY-EIGHT

KYLE PULLED THE rental into the lot and reported the damage—just a streak of red paint on the right front fender. He claimed he kissed a pole while backing out of a parking lot. No matter, he'd used a false identity when signing for the car and had paid for full-coverage insurance. The hat and sunglasses, even if a camera filmed him returning the vehicle, made for a solid disguise. He looked like a million guys.

He sauntered a few blocks away and caught a cab. By the time he arrived back at his car and drove home, his nephews were ready for a late afternoon fishing trip at Ile d'Orleans, only a short drive away.

"Jon," he called. "Pack the poles and gear. I've loaded a cooler with drinks and nabbed some snacks while I was out earlier."

"Martin? Are you ready?"

The ten-year-old stampeded down the stairs. "Past ready."

Kyle hung his arm over the kid's shoulder and

gave him a squeeze. "You remind me of myself when I was a kid. Always ready for adventure."

Jon gazed at him with a proud grin.

CHAPTER THIRTY-NINE

I CONVINCED MCGRATH to bring us takeout from the diner on the corner near the hotel. Eating another bite of hospital food would not speed my recovery. If I were going to build up my strength so the doctor would sign my release, I required sustenance, and fast. When he pulled a surprise bottle of Cabernet from his duffle bag, I almost whooped with joy, but didn't want to draw attention to our private celebration. Plus, the hospital staff might frown on the presence of alcohol in a patient's room.

"Did Ben take wine to Katharine's room?"

"He did. They moved her to a regular floor. She's no longer in the ICU. Sounds like they might let her go tomorrow, too. Her nurse told Ben she's making a great recovery. Things look great since her surgery and her doc at home can check on the pins and screws they inserted by taking an X-ray in a week or so. They're happy to forward her records."

"What a relief."

"You seem at peace with the two lovebirds."

"They'll sort things out. Katharine spoke to Paul earlier. He's busy, so she'll see him when she gets home."

"I'd like to talk to you about something else." His expression turned grave and his eyes bored into me.

"What's wrong?"

"Nothing, but I wanted you to know something. I phoned Lucas Sweeney."

"You did?" I chewed the inside of my cheek. This could go one of several ways. When McGrath was shot and began suffering amnesia, he'd become uncharacteristically easy-going. I wagered a guess those carefree days were over. And when he spoke again, a gritty edge to his voice, I understood why.

"Yes, and he seemed quite aware of your determination to contact Judy Culver. He also mentioned Judy's half-brother, Stitsill's son, who's in his late twenties and has chosen to follow in his father's footsteps."

I squirmed in my seat and sipped my wine, "That makes me a bit nervous. I mean, I know Stitsill spread around his sperm like broad-spectrum fertilizer, but to think of his kid doing what his dad did is unnerving, to say the least."

"Anyway, he wanted me to tell you he's on the guy's trail, and not to worry. They should close in on him any time now."

"Close in on him. What does that mean? You're saying we have nothing to worry about, but the powers that be are hunting for the guy?"

"I understand this puts you on edge. But Sweeney's an expert and I'm sure he has a team of professionals taking care of business. Still, I don't want you out of my sight. We've been through enough of these nail biters. I'm spending the night here. With you."

"All we need is some deviant offspring of Stitsill's interfering with our lives. But think about it. I'm in a hospital. There's tons of staff in and out of my room. This has to be a safe place."

McGrath tipped his head toward the vase on my tray table. "You received an arrangement of flowers from an anonymous admirer on the heels of being run down on the streets while visiting a strange city. Have you completely lost your mind?"

Yes, my darling detective had regained his persona as well as his memory. Headstrong, pigheaded, stubborn McGrath was back.

"Listen, Detective, I hear you loud and clear. But I am far past letting some kid intimidate me. Giving in to fear is letting him win. I'd rather face him and give him a piece of my mind."

"That's fine, just count on me to be here to watch."

"Yes, sir."

His lips curved into a smile and those damned dimples of his deepened.

***

We fell asleep some time after ten. McGrath first—his soft snores were loud enough I could no longer hear the TV, so I flicked off the set to join him. But first, I gazed at him for a few minutes. As the soft light and shadows danced across his face, I studied his square jaw and his slightly crooked nose, his bushy eyebrows. I loved his ruggedness, his Adam's apple, the shadow of stubble growing across his cheeks and chin.

If Jon was looking down on me, he'd want me to be with this kind of man. Someone who loved me unconditionally—a solid guy who was as protective and caring of me as he was of my children. He'd flinch a tad at the sex thing, to put it mildly, but if he were in my shoes, my guess was he wouldn't have waited as long as I had to even consider the possibility.

I drifted off to sleep counting my innumerable blessings. What seemed like mere minutes later, I awoke to a shadow looming above me. In nightmares, I had always imagined a moment like this, where I was staring death in the eye and unable to scream. I'd open my mouth, but nothing would come out, just a silent, horrified breath.

Miraculously, I did scream this time, and loud enough to awaken McGrath, who leapt over me, tackled the intruder, restrained him in a headlock, and nailed him to the floor within seconds.

"It's me," a strangled voice rose from the ground. "Ben."

Several hospital staff burst through the door, illuminating the room with a flip of the switch and filling the area around my bed with chatter and commotion. McGrath's fist was still raised over Ben, poised to land a punch as the crowd ensued. He dropped his arm and helped Ben to his feet, brushing himself off.

"You're a force to be reckoned with, my friend," Ben joked. "You're lucky I'm non-violent. Tai Chi is a form of martial art I practice for health benefits, but I could have taken you out with one simple kick."

A nurse barked, "Everyone out. We can't have this kind of activity taking place in patient's room. People are trying to sleep." Then, she spun around and instructed one of the other staff standing behind her. "Call security."

Figures. The one time we get an English-speaking nurse, we'd rather not.

The woman rushed out of the room, and the other two nurse's aides stood sentry beside the door.

"Hold on. There's been some kind of mistake," I said. "These are my friends. We had a simple misunderstanding," I tried to explain. "We were both—"

"I don't care what happened," her voice rose and became more commanding with every word as she narrowed a vicious gaze at Ben and then McGrath, pointing her finger like a teacher chastising two misbehaving students. "You leave this very minute. No explanations or excuses. If you don't want an armed escort, you'll do what I ask without another word."

"Wait, please," I pleaded.

Her gaze bore into me. "Ma'am," she said. "You have no voice here."

That shut me up.

Her eyes shot back to Ben and McGrath. "Gentlemen?"

Two armed guards entered the room.

McGrath whispered to me, "I'll be back as soon as I have a chance to reason with these guys."

"No worries. They'll definitely be watching my room closely now." I eked out a pained half-smile.

One security guard opened the door while the other gestured for everyone to leave. The charge nurse indicated that Ben and McGrath should lead the way. In an instant, the entourage marched out of the room, but the tension built in those few minutes hung heavy in the air—a threatening storm cloud. I struggled to ease the pressure weighing on my chest.

Minutes later the pain in my broken limbs rose to an intolerable high. I called the nurse and requested pain medication, only to be met by her harsh glare after a good long wait. Her footsteps echoed on the tile as she tromped between my monitors and the IV pole.

I resisted the urge to ask what she was injecting into my arm. She was one scary lady.

CHAPTER FORTY

SHAKEN OUT OF a deep sleep, I peered at the evil nurse who had kicked McGrath and Ben out of my room. The room was dark, with only a sliver of light peeking out from beneath the bathroom door, but I recognized her beady little eyes and brusque bedside manner. I couldn't imagine what was so important that she'd wake me in the middle of the night.

"Mrs. Stitsill," she hissed. "Your son is here to see you."

I was confused. Nick? Will? Which one? And how did they get to Quebec? Had I drifted into a coma and lost a couple of days?

She clomped out of the room. I blinked several times, my mind dulled by sleep and medication.

"Nick?" I said. "Is that you?"

A figure moved towards me, taller and thinner than my Nick, but not so dissimilar from Will. But Will hated hospitals—he would rather chew the bark off a tree than see me like this. "Will?"

A hand went over my mouth, pushing my head up and into the pillow. Another hand slid beneath my head and lifted me. Instinct kicked in. I wriggled up in bed. My crisis prevention training booted up. I repeated the mantra in my head. "Move with your attacker rather than resisting the attack." At the same time, I lifted my broken arm and slammed the cast against the form bearing down on me.

I heard a sickening smack, but the compression on my face didn't lessen, rather fingers slipped around my throat. He pulled me from the bed and closed his hands around my throat. Somehow I was able to bear weight on my bad leg and twist into him, catching him off guard. I set my casted arm on his back and bore down, adrenaline shooting through me as I kneed him in the groin.

"Goddamn bastard. You will not hurt me."

He fell backward, writhing in pain.

I raced into the hall, shouting, "Help! Help me!"

The evil nurse appeared. "What the …?"

I was knocked to the ground from behind and dragged back toward my room.

"Stop right there," the nurse ordered. She came at us like a crazed animal, climbing onto the two of us, grabbing the man's hair and pulling.

"Kick him," she screamed. "Fight!"

I was fighting all right—for breath. For my heart to restart. Wedged between the two of them, I could hardly move.

"Get off," I yelled. "Go get help."

But she was relentless—kicking, scrambling, scratching—now on her feet and dragging me from his grasp. We both slid to the floor. A loudspeaker sounded in the hall and blue lights began to flash. "Code bleu. Code bleu."

Footsteps sounded in the hall. The nurse and I were on the floor, I spotted her shoe and blue scrubs to the left of me. I struggled to scramble away from the madman, belly crawling with my one good arm and leg, fighting the weight of the casts on the opposite side of my body, along with the haphazard sliding complication they presented as I wrestled to get away. A hand gripped my bad ankle, tugging me, then dragging me across the floor.

A thought raced through my head. *Don't let him take you back in the room.*

Visions of my kids, their school photos, for some bizarre reason, flashed through my brain. McGrath's dimples. Is this what it's like right before you die? *There's no fucking way this guy is getting the better of me.*

A booming voice called, "Stop right there!" Sounded like the security guard.

I could barely see, stuck on my back, between the wall and the group of hospital staff who seemed to be trying to trap the assailant, another nurse now yanking on my arm as the crazy man wrenched on my leg.

Pain screamed through my limbs. I twisted and writhed, catching the hem of the security guard's pant leg, the scuff of his black shoes at the edge of my vision. *Please be skilled.*

My foot came free as my assailant either let go or was pulled away, I couldn't tell which. I rolled onto my side in time to see him scuffle with the security guard, the gun the guard was wielding causing the nurses to flee inside the nearest open door and hide. Within an instant, only my attacker, the guard, and I were left at the end of the hall in front of my room door. I scrambled into the corner, semi-crouching, trying to stand in order to somehow get away, save myself.

The guard and the assailant continued to tussle, landing blows. Groans and guttural sounds erupted from the men as they landed sharp blows on each other. I peered to my left, searching for a handrail, some way to lift myself up, when I spotted the guard's gun, two feet away from me on the floor. I reached the weapon with my fingertips, grasped the grip in my hand and positioned myself in the corner again, lining up for a direct shot at the attacker, but then dropping the firearm to my lap. Think, Sam. Think.

The security guard was running out of steam and reinforcements were nowhere to be seen. Another punch cracked the guard's nose. His head hit the floor hard, and blood gushed from his face.

The man sat on the guard's chest now, ready to

land another punch on the now unconscious man. He'd kill him if I didn't step in. He'd kill me next.

Blue lights continued to flash as I combed the hall once more—praying for a miracle, praying for cops, praying for guidance.

My gaze shot back to the two men. The assailant stood, seeing me again—the sudden recognition causing him to sneer and assume a stance, like a caged fighter, nearly dancing in front of me.

He lurched forward.

Boom! Boom! Boom!

Footsteps stampeded toward me.

My head fell to my chest. I left my body.

CHAPTER FORTY-ONE

I AWOKE IN a hospital room, McGrath at my side, stroking my hand and delivering a gentle message, "You did good, kid. You're going to be okay."

My head throbbed like I'd been over-served several days in a row. I couldn't keep my stomach from lurching or my pulse from pounding in my ears.

"What happened?"

"Just rest now. Close your eyes and try to sleep. There's nothing to worry about."

"I don't understand."

"I know." McGrath soothed me with his words. "But you will. Later."

Exhaustion crept through every cell in my body, like an impenetrable fog, clouding my brain as well.

"I can't sleep until I know. Are you okay? Is Katharine? Where are the kids? The nurse said Nick was here. Or was it Will?"

"The kids are fine, Sam. They're Up North with Ed. I talked to them just this morning. They're fishing today and are anxious to see us whenever we manage to make the trip. Ed said to take our time. We aren't expected back for a few more weeks anyway. Plenty of time for you to get back on your feet."

"Where's Ben? You hit him, didn't you?"

"He's a forgiving man. And I didn't hit him, just tackled him to the ground."

"I hope he'll let you back into the museum. Wait. You remembered everything, didn't you?" I tried sitting up in bed, but I was overcome by spasms shooting down my leg.

"Hard to know if I've remembered everything. I don't know what I forgot. But I do know this. We met a couple of years ago. I fell totally, madly, puppy-dog in love with you the moment I laid eyes on you, and last night you agreed to marry me. What I'm most concerned about though, is that you remember saying yes."

Oxygen filled my lungs. "I remember."

"Take a nap, and we'll make plans when you wake up."

CHAPTER FORTY-TWO

TWO DAYS LATER, I crutched my way to the recliner and eased myself down. The window blinds were opened, and I absorbed the view—blue skies with wisps of long flat clouds swept upon them, the sun's rays streaming in swaths across the horizon.

My stomach rumbled. For the first time in days, I was hungry.

Lucas Sweeney filled the doorway a second later, having tapped on the door and opening it simultaneously. He cut a handsome figure—tall, trim, as neatly bearded as I remembered him, but with significantly shorter hair. His angular nose and wise brown eyes spoke volumes, etched with sympathy as they were.

"Hey," I said.

Lucas pulled up a chair and took my hand. "Good to see you, Sam."

"I'm guessing you're the person who's going to tell me what happened. Jim is protective and insists I rest. He wants me out of this place, and soon."

"You can't blame the guy for taking care of you. From what I understand, you're about to be his bride. Congratulations."

"We've finally taken the next step."

Lucas leaned forward. "Jon would be happy for you, Sam. He loved you and the kids more than words can say. He spoke of you with such pride, all you accomplished in bringing your two families together and creating such a tight knit group. On his behalf, I bequeath his blessing."

"Ha," I said. "You have this way about you, Lucas. And I want so much to believe you, I think I will. Now, stop stalling and tell me what happened. Who was trying to kill me and why?"

"Stitsill had a son. His name was Kyle and he'd recently succeeded in assuming a more active role with the organization his father worked for on some occasions."

"You'd tell me the name of the group, but then you'd have to kill me, right?"

His eyes smiled, a look of recognition riding on their heels. "The kid figured out you and McGrath were involved in his dad's death. He was young. A hothead. Figured he was skilled enough and man enough to close the circle. He'd killed before, and with no great pains. His half-sister, Judy Carver, is the woman you called on earlier in your visit. She's since shared some details with me, about his childhood and recent years. While she didn't know all of the particulars, between what she knew and we were able to piece together, the kid had a tough childhood, a learning disability which was never dealt with, and a sociopathic personality which was never treated."

"My heart goes out to kids like him. So many have crossed my path. I know it's silly and altruistic of me to believe so, but whenever I hear tragic tales like this, I always think if I could have been the kid's teacher, I could have turned him around. My friend Jack always says, 'You can't save 'em all, Stitsill,'but I'd sure like to try."

"Your friend Jack sounds like a solid advisor."

"In essence, this poor kid wanted me dead as revenge for his father's death."

"In a nutshell, yes. Trust me, you did the world a favor by getting him off the streets. And in your case, you're lucky."

"Not feeling too lucky at the moment. I killed a young, troubled man."

"You saved yourself, and probably a throng of other folks."

I swallowed hard and my wrung my hands. "I'll learn to live with my actions, but I'll also question my decisions. For as long as I live. Hell, I can't even let myself off the hook for forgetting to sign a permission slips for one of my kids'field trips."

"Give yourself time, Sam. And know how responsible I feel for putting you in a position where you had to be the one to pull the trigger. We had Stitsill in our sights, but he slipped past us. You'd think we'd be more skilled by now."

"I've killed three people now, but those deaths are on me, not you."

"You've touched hundreds of lives. Life dealt you a wicked hand. A lesser person would have left five kids orphaned."

He had a valid point.

"What about me? Will I be able to leave Canada without being arrested?"

"I'm sure the local police will be in to talk to you, but Mrs. Wright, the nurse who was caring for you the night of the incident, and Officer Swanson, the guard whose life you saved, have both given the authorities enough information for them to understand you were acting in self-defense."

"I'm confused about how this guy got past security and into my room. I have this fuzzy memory of the nurse bringing him into my room late at night."

"He waltzed up to the nurse's desk at 3 A.M. and showed Mrs. Wright his driver's license, a U.S. license with his name, Kyle Stitsill. Claimed to be your son, and gave her a sob story about how he'd driven for hours to be at your side. She thought he was legit."

I let out a breath, the weight of the past few days escaping with the air. "You're right. I'm lucky to be alive."

"That's all of them, now. No other surviving Stitsill family member harbors any ill will toward you. They had been coping with Kyle for years, mostly Judy, unequipped as she was to deal with a mentally ill brother. As long as you can stay out of trouble, which in your case seems to be a tremendous challenge, you should experience smooth roads. Keep your nose clean.

"I should head out, Sam, but as always, I've enjoyed seeing you."

Lucas stood and leaned down to give me a quick hug. Most people wouldn't understand, but Jon's touch came through in Sweeney's embrace. I was consumed with peace and contentment.

"Thank you, Lucas. You're a treasured friend."

His wise eyes told me he felt the same.

"If you'll accept an email, I'll invite you to the wedding."

"Great. I'll look forward to it."

I sank back in my chair. Life might work out after all.

CHAPTER FORTY-TWO

I LOST TRACK of time staring out the window, not seeing anything, adrift in a sea of thoughts. Wedding dates, whom to invite, where to hold the ceremony. How to include the kids. Send a letter to my boss, rescinding my request for a leave. Paul. Ben. Katharine.

A knock on the door interrupted my thoughts. "Mrs. Stitsill?"

I answered from my chair. "Yes?"

"You have a visitor."

The door opened and a nurse wheeled in Katharine. My face lit up seeing my friend. I reached for her and the nurse positioned her near enough for me to hold her hand.

Drawn and thin with a gray pallor, she asked, "How are you?"

"No," I said, "how are you?"

She offered a weak smile, her uncertainty barely hidden.

"Physically, I'm improving every day. Because

you were staying an extra few days, the emergency for me to be released faded to the background. But emotionally, I'm a wreck."

I stroked her hand and held her gaze. "Tell me."

"It's Ben. I love him. I always have. How do I change that? How do I go back to Paul? The time is fast approaching. I can't not go home, tempting as the idea of riding off into oblivion with Ben is. I have a life in Bar Harbor."

"It's funny, you know. When Jim lost his memory, I had moments when I envied him. This giant eraser takes away not only memories, but also the feelings—guilt, recriminations, pain, shame, self-doubt. The heartaches are gone in a flash. But then, I realized how every moment of my past makes me who I am today. Not that I didn't comprehend the 'I am a culmination of everything I've done before', but I understood in a different way.

"What makes us unique is not just what happens to us, but the way we handle things. In crisis, I've always powered through, and then fallen apart later, but I've also backed myself into a corner, always been the helper, rather than ever allowing anyone else in. I've protected myself from hurt, but at the same time, eradicated any chance of being truly in love, truly *with* someone.

"Jon traveled all the time, I had to stay afloat at all costs, so I did everything myself. No one could handle things as well as me. No one could juggle a million tasks and not drop a single ball. But I could. Then the loneliness stepped in. But I'd trapped myself. Not only did I believe I could do it all, Jon believed it too. When I told him I was desperate for his company, he patted me on the back and promised he'd be home soon. He thought I was having a moment, but I was having a year—a year that grew into two years, then three.

"If he'd lived, I often wonder if we would still be married. Don't get me wrong. Jon was a great guy. He was a good provider and when he was home, he did his best to pay attention. But his best wasn't good enough, and I never had the courage to tell him."

I stopped and stared at a mottled square of tile.

"I have no idea what I'm saying with this soliloquy. But here's the one thing I do know. Life is shorter than I ever imagined. My kids will be grown and gone before I can clap my hands, my father-in-law could fall ill tomorrow. But I'm here today with a man who loves me. I'm ready to give myself to him, more completely than I've ever imagined. It won't be easy, I'm sure I'll rely on old familiar habits in spite of myself, but I'm bound and determined to be happy and love richly. I'm promising myself now, to do my very best.

"I want you to do the same. Take a stand for you. Not for Ben. Not for Paul. But for Katharine. Life's too short to do anything less."

She reached for me, and, as best we could, we

held each other tight.

CHAPTER FORTY-THREE

M CGRATH PULLED THE car to the curb, then rushed around to help me inside. For once, the crutches were more friends than enemies, but loading myself in and out of vehicles was still a minor challenge. Once situated in the passenger seat, I handed him the staves and waited for him to assume his spot as my delectable chauffeur.

Katharine and Ben loaded into the car behind us.

We would caravan back to Maine. Katharine and I, alone with our secret goals and desires, were ready to journey this new road we'd both promised each other we'd make a decent attempt to pass.

I peered over my shoulder, unable to see her, but aware she was thinking of me, as I was of her.

"Can Katharine see me?" I asked McGrath.

"She's facing forward if that's any help."

"Thanks," I said as I gave her a thumbs up.

"Ready?" McGrath's eyes were alight with deep affection, and he played with the ring finger of my left hand.

"More than ready.

www.ingramcontent.com/pod-product-compliance
Lightning Source LLC
Chambersburg PA
CBHW071104250626
47159CB00002B/594